"Someone else has been here recently."

Josiah pointed  shoe print a... thirteen size...

"A man? Someone else searching for the kids?"

His gut clenched. "Maybe one of the counselors came this way." Or maybe it was someone else who had nothing to do with the day camp. He wouldn't voice that to Ella. She didn't need to worry any more than she already was.

Josiah continued after Buddy. The dog stopped at the base of a spruce tree, sniffing the trunk, then taking off to the left.

Ella's wide brown eyes riveted on him. "I saw the lengthening of the spaces between the footprints. Robbie was running, wasn't he?"

Her gaze drew him in, so much pain reflected in it. He gritted his teeth, not wanting to answer her question, not wanting to add to her distress.

"You don't have to say anything. I can see it on your face. Something or someone scared him. The person whose boot prints we found with his. I saw them under the tree, too. He's being stalked."

Margaret Daley, an award-winning author of ninety books (five million sold worldwide), has been married for over forty years and is a firm believer in romance and love. When she isn't traveling, she's writing love stories, often with a suspense thread, and corralling her three cats that think they rule her household. To find out more about Margaret visit her website at margaretdaley.com.

Books by Margaret Daley

Love Inspired Suspense

Alaskan Search and Rescue Series

The Yuletide Rescue
To Save Her Child

Guardians Inc. Series

Christmas Bodyguard
Protecting Her Own
Hidden in the Everglades
Christmas Stalking
Guarding the Witness
Bodyguard Reunion

Visit the Author Profile page at Harlequin.com for more titles.

TO SAVE
HER CHILD

MARGARET DALEY

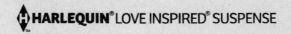

HARLEQUIN® LOVE INSPIRED® SUSPENSE

Recycling programs
for this product may
not exist in your area.

LOVE INSPIRED BOOKS

ISBN-13: 978-0-373-44648-3

To Save Her Child

Copyright © 2015 by Margaret Daley

This edition published by arrangement with Love Inspired Books.

® and TM are trademarks of Love Inspired Books, used under license.
Trademarks indicated with ® are registered in the United States Patent
and Trademark Office, the Canadian Intellectual Property Office and in
other countries.

www.Harlequin.com

Printed in U.S.A.

If God is for us, who can be against us?
—Romans 8:31

To all my readers—thank you for choosing my book

ONE

Ella Jackson looked longingly at the black leather couch against the far wall in her office. If only she could close her eyes for an hour—even half an hour—she would be ready to tackle the rest of the data entry for the upcoming Northern Frontier Search and Rescue training weekend.

She trudged to her desk, staring at the stack of papers she needed to work her way through before picking up her eight-year-old son from day camp, then heading home. She should have been finished by now, but in the middle of the night a search and rescue call had gone out for an elderly gentleman. She had manned the command center for his search, which had ended with the man being found, but her exhaustion from lack of sleep was finally catching up with her.

When she saw her son, Robbie, he would no doubt have a ton of questions about the emergency that had sent him to her neighbor's. This wasn't the first time she'd disturbed her son's sleep in the middle of the night because of a search and rescue, and Robbie was a trooper. Once he'd come with her to the command center when she couldn't find a babysitter. He'd begged to go with her ever since then, but it was impossible to watch over him and fulfill her duties. She'd promised him when he was older, he could.

The sight of the training folder on the desktop screen taunted her to get to work. David Stone, who ran the organization, would return soon and need the list, since the instructional exercises would take place in two days. So much to get done before Saturday. As she sat in her desk chair, she rubbed her blurry eyes, then clicked on the folder. The schedule and list popped up, the cursor blinking hypnotically. When her head started dropping forward, she jerked it up. Not even two pots of coffee were helping her to stay alert.

The door into the hangar opened, and her boss entered. He'd conducted the aerial search for Mr. Otterman, who had finally been found wandering in the middle of a shallow stream two miles from his nursing home.

Her gaze connected with David's. "Mr. Otterman checked out fine, according to your wife, and he's safely back at Aurora Nursing Home."

"Thankfully Josiah and Alex got to him before he made it to the river the stream fed into." He looked as tired as she felt. "Josiah is right behind me. Send him into my office when he comes in."

For a few seconds, Ella was sidetracked by the mention of Josiah. There was something about the man that intrigued her. His short black hair, the bluest eyes she'd ever seen and a slender, athletic build set her heart racing. Although he was handsome, she'd learned to be leery of men with those kinds of looks. No, it was his presence at a search and rescue that drew her to him. Commanding, captivating—and a loner. She knew one when she met one because she was much more comfortable alone, especially after her marriage to an abusive man. For a second, thoughts of her ex-husband threatened to take hold. She wouldn't go there. He'd done enough to her in the past. She wouldn't allow him—even in memories—into her present life.

"Ella, are you all right?"

David pulled her away from her thoughts. "I'm okay. Bree wanted me to tell you to go home and get some sleep since you never went to bed last night."

"My wife worries too much. Josiah and I need to work out some details about the training this weekend." David studied her. "But *you* should definitely go home. You were here before I was this morning."

"But these lists—"

The jarring ring of the phone cut off the rest of Ella's sentence. She snatched it up and said, "Northern Frontier Search and Rescue. How may I help you?"

"Mrs. Jackson?" a female voice asked.

It sounded like one of the counselors at the day camp Robbie went to during the summer. "Yes. Is this Stacy?"

"Yes. I'm so sorry to call you, but your son and two other boys are missing. We've looked everywhere around here and can't find them. We'll continue—"

"What happened?" Stunned, Ella gripped the phone tighter. Surely she'd misheard.

"We don't know. Robbie, Travis and Michael were playing together during free time between activities, but when the counselor rounded up everyone for the Alaskan bear presentation, they were gone."

"I'll be right there with some help to search for them." She didn't know how she managed to speak a coherent sentence, her mouth was as dry as the desert. Phone still in her trembling hand, Ella rose, glancing around for her purse. Where did she put it?

"I'd hoped you would say that. It's not like them to run off."

"I'll be there as soon as possible." She nearly dropped the phone as she looked around trying to find her leather bag. Beads of perspiration broke out on her forehead. Usually it was on the floor under the desk near her feet.

Where is it? I need my keys. The camp wouldn't call me unless...

Her heartbeat raced. Tears pooled in her eyes. She put the phone in its cradle, and then rummaged through her desk drawers.

David clasped her arms and forced her to stop her search. "What's wrong?"

"It's Robbie. He's missing from Camp Yukon with two other boys."

David released his grasp and reached toward the filing cabinet. "Here's your purse." He put it in her hand.

She hugged her handbag against her chest, then started for the door.

"Wait, Ella. Let me make some calls. We'll get volunteers out to the campsite. Josiah is still out in the hangar with his dog, Buddy. Catch him before his sister leaves. She was heading out to her car when I came in. Have one of them drive you. You shouldn't go by yourself, and it might take me some time to get the search organized and notify the authorities in case the camp hasn't."

As though on autopilot, Ella changed directions and headed to the hangar, scanning the cavernous area for Josiah Witherspoon and his search and rescue German shepherd. They had just been successful in finding Mr. Otterman. But then she thought back to the ones they hadn't found in time. *Not my son. Please, God. Not my son.*

Ella spied Josiah coming into the open hangar from outside, Buddy, a black-and-brown German shepherd on a leash next to him. He walked toward her, his long strides quickly cutting the distance between them.

"What's wrong, Ella?" His tanned forehead scrunched and his dark blue eyes filled with concern. "Another job?"

Words stuck in her throat. She nodded, fighting the tears welling in her. "My son is missing," she finally squeaked out.

"Where? When?" he asked, suddenly all business.

"About an hour ago at Camp Yukon, which is held at Kincaid Park near the outdoor center. They did a preliminary search but couldn't find him or the two boys with him. David said—" She swallowed several times. "I hope you can help look for them."

Josiah was already retrieving his cell phone from his belt clip. "I'll let Alex know to go there. She just left with her dog, Sadie." He connected with his twin sister and gave her the information. "I'll be right behind you. I'm bringing Ella," he told her. Then he hung up.

"You don't have to. I can…" She gripped her purse's straps tighter, the leather digging into her palms. Robbie was all she had. *I can't lose him, Lord.* "Thanks. It's probably wiser if I don't drive."

"Let's go. My truck is outside." Josiah fell into step next to her.

Ella slid a glance toward him, and the sight of Josiah, a former US Marine, calmed her nerves. She knew how good he and his sister were with their dogs at finding people. Robbie would be all right. She had to believe that. The alternative was unthinkable. She shuddered.

On the passenger side he opened the back door for Buddy, then quickly moved to the front door for Ella. "I'll find Robbie. I promise."

The confidence in his voice further eased her anxiety and momentarily held the cold at bay. Ella climbed into the F-150 extended cab with Josiah's hand on her elbow, as if he was letting her know he would be here for her. She appreciated it, but at the moment she felt as though she was barely holding herself together. She couldn't fall apart because Robbie would need her when they found him. He was probably more frightened than she was. Once, when he was five, they had been separated in a department store, and when she'd found him a minute later, he had been sitting on the floor, crying.

As Josiah started the engine, Ella hugged her arms to her and ran her hands up and down them. But the chill had returned and burrowed its way into the marrow of her bones, even though the temperature was sixty-five degrees and the sun streamed through the truck's windshield, heating up the interior.

Josiah glanced at her. "David will get enough people to scour the whole park."

"But so many just came off working Mr. Otterman's disappearance."

"That won't stop us. There are three lost boys. Do you have anything with Robbie's scent on it?"

"I do. In my car."

He backed up to her ten-year-old black Jeep Wrangler. "Where?"

"Front seat. A jacket he didn't take with him to the babysitter last night." Ella grasped the handle. The weatherman had mentioned the temperatures overnight would dip down into the forties, and all Robbie was wearing was a thin shirt.

"I'll get it." Josiah jumped out of the truck before Ella had a chance to even open her door.

She watched him move to her car. She'd only known Josiah and his sister for six months, since they'd begun volunteering for Northern Frontier Search and Rescue, but they'd quickly become invaluable to the organization. Alex had lived here for years, whereas Josiah had only recently left the Marines. They were co-owners of Outdoor Alaska, a company that outfitted search and rescue teams and wilderness enthusiasts.

Although he was a large man, she'd seen Josiah move with an agility that surprised her. He returned with Robbie's brown jacket in his grasp.

He gave it to Ella. "This will help Buddy find your son."

The bright light of a few minutes ago began to fade. Ella leaned forward, staring out the windshield at the sky. Dark clouds drifted over the sun. "Looks like we'll have a storm late this afternoon."

When Josiah flowed into the traffic on Minnesota

Drive, an expressway that bisected Anchorage, his strong jawline twitched. "We can still search in the rain, but let's hope we find them beforehand or that the weatherman is wrong."

Ella leaned her head against the headrest and closed her eyes. She had to remain calm and in control. That was one of the things she'd always been able to do in the middle of a search and rescue, but this time it was her son. Now she knew firsthand what the families of the missing people went through. The thundering beat of her heart clamored against her chest, and the rate of her breathing increased. Sweat beaded on her forehead, and she scrubbed her hand across her face.

"Ella, I won't leave the park until we find the boys."

"There are a lot of trees and animals in the park. What if he runs into a bear or even a moose? They could..." She refused to think of what could happen. *Remain calm.* But no matter how much she repeated that to herself, she couldn't.

"How old is your son?"

"Eight."

"Has he had any survival training in the outdoors?"

"A little. One of the reasons I signed him up for the day camp was to start some of that. We've made a few excursions but haven't camped overnight anywhere." Robbie was timid and afraid of everything. If she'd left her ex-husband sooner, her son might not be so scared of loud noises, or the dark. At least Robbie wasn't alone and it was still light outside.

"We'll be there soon."

In the distance Ella glimpsed Ted Stevens Anchorage International Airport, which was north of the park. Maybe the counselors had found Robbie by now. Then she realized that they would have called her if they had. She checked her cell phone to make sure the ringer's volume was up.

Josiah exited the highway, and at an intersection he slanted a look toward her that made Ella feel as though he were sending her some of his strength and calmness. "Thank you for bringing me."

"Remember how successful we were at locating Mr. Otterman? The park is big, but it is surrounded on two sides with water and one with the airport. The area is contained."

"But it's fourteen hundred acres. That's a huge area to cover."

"Can he swim?"

Ella swiped a few stray stands of her blond hair back from her face. "Yes, but why do you ask?"

"I'm just trying to get a sense of what Robbie knows how to do since the park has water and Cook Inlet butts up against it."

"He loves to fish, so I made sure he learned to swim at an early age."

"I love to fish. Nothing beats a fresh-caught salmon."

Ella rubbed her thumb into her palm over and over. "That's how the bears feel, too. What if he runs into one and forgets everything he's been taught?" Her heartbeat raced even more at the thought.

Josiah turned onto Raspberry Road. "If he doesn't run from one and makes noise as he walks, he should be okay. Neither one wants to be surprised. I'm sure the first day the counselors went over how to behave in the wilderness."

"Yes, but…"

Josiah slowed and threw her a look full of understanding. "You've dealt with family members when someone is lost, like Mr. Otterman's son and daughter-in-law earlier today. I've seen you. You always seem to be able to reassure them. Think about the words you tell them and repeat them to yourself."

"I pray with them. I tell them about the people who are looking for their loved one. How good they are at what they do."

"Exactly." Josiah tossed his head toward the backseat of the cab. "Buddy is good at locating people. I know how to track people through a forest. Tell you what—I'll start the prayer. You can add whatever you want."

As Josiah began his prayer for Robbie, something shifted inside Ella. The tight knot in her stomach began to unravel.

"Lord, I know Your power and love. Anything is possible through You. Please help Buddy and me find Robbie and the other two boys safe and unharmed." Josiah's truck entered the park, and he glanced at her.

"And please bless the ones searching for my son and his friends. Comfort the families and friends who are waiting. Amen," Ella finished, seeing Josiah in a new light today. They'd talked casually the past few months, but there was always a barrier there, a look of pain in his blue eyes. She knew that expression because she fought to keep hers hidden since she dealt with so many people who needed someone to listen to them when they were hurting. She could help them, but she wasn't sure anyone could help her.

In the woods, Josiah gave Buddy as much leash as possible and let him dictate where they went. Having insisted she couldn't stay at the command post, Ella trailed behind him as they searched farther away from the base at the day camp. His sister and her dog, Sadie, were following Travis's scent, while another search and rescue worker, Jesse Hunt, had the third boy's backpack, and his dog was tracking that child.

Josiah glanced over at Alex to his right and Jesse to his left, both within ten feet of him. Suddenly the dogs veered away from each other. Buddy went straight while the others made an almost ninety-degree turn.

"They separated?" Ella asked, coming up to his side.

"I believe so." Tearing his gaze away from her fearful eyes, Josiah examined the soft ground. "Someone else has been here recently." He pointed to the ground. "That's Robbie's shoe print and that's someone with a size twelve or thirteen boot."

"A man? Someone else searching for the kids?"

His gut clenched. "Maybe one of the counselors came this way." Or maybe it was someone else who had nothing to do with the day camp. He wouldn't voice that to Ella. She didn't need to worry any more than she already was.

Josiah continued following Buddy, scanning the ground for any signs that would help him find Robbie. He didn't know how Ella could deal with the people who waited to see if their family member or friend was found. While bringing her to Kincaid Park, he'd felt unsure of what to say to help her. He was used to being alone. He was better off working alone with Buddy. He'd learned that the hard way.

Buddy stopped at the base of a spruce tree, sniffing the trunk, then taking off to the left. Josiah inspected the lower branches and found a few of the smaller ones were broken off—recently.

"I believe he climbed this tree." Josiah pointed at the damaged limbs, then headed the direction Buddy went.

"If only he'd stayed here. It's been hours since he disappeared. It's starting to get colder, and he has no jacket on." Falling into step next to Josiah, Ella scanned the dense woods surrounding them.

The quaver in her voice penetrated the hard shell he'd placed his emotions in to put his life back together after being a prisoner of war in the Middle East. "He's walked and even run a long way from where he was last seen. He'll get tired and probably find a place to rest."

Ella's wide brown eyes were riveted to his. "What made them separate? I saw the lengthening of the spaces between the footprints. He was running then, wasn't he?"

Her gaze drew him in, so much pain reflected in it. He gritted his teeth, not wanting to answer her question, not wanting to add to her distress.

"You don't have to say anything. I can see it on your face. Something or someone scared him. The person whose boot prints we found with his. I saw them under the tree, too. He's being stalked." Ella came to stop.

"It could be someone searching for the kids. Don't jump to any conclusions. Speculation can drive you crazy."

"Just the facts, then. We're on point on this search. The rest are spread out and going much slower behind us." Her teeth dug into her lower lip.

Before he realized what he was doing, he touched her shoulder, feeling the tension beneath his fingers. "Let's go. We don't need to stand around speculating." He squeezed her gently before he turned toward Buddy, who was sniffing the ground five yards away.

His dog barked and charged forward, straining against the leash. Five minutes later, Buddy weaved through some trees, yelping several times. Josiah kept pace with his dog, his body screaming in protest at the long hours he'd been awake without much rest. His German shepherd circled a patch of ground.

Josiah came to a halt at the spot with Ella next to him. She stared at the ground, her face pale. Bear prints. Fresh ones.

"A bear is nearby, possibly after Robbie," Ella whispered in a squeaky voice, her eyes huge.

TWO

Ella sucked in a deep breath that she held until pain shot through her chest. Finally she exhaled, then managed to ask, "Is the bear following him?"

"No, but it looks as though Robbie stopped, turned around, then began running this way." Josiah pointed to the right. "The bear is going straight."

"Oh, good." Relief sagged her shoulders until she realized the bear might not be the only one.

After taking his dog off the leash, Josiah signaled to Buddy to continue tracking Robbie. As Josiah followed behind the German shepherd, he said over his shoulder, "I think Robbie is slowing down. His strides are closer together."

Her cell phone rang, and Ella quickly answered it. It was David. "Has anyone been found?"

"Yes, Travis."

Ella said a quick prayer of thanks.

David continued. "Alex located him not far from Little Campbell Lake. She's bringing him in."

"Did he tell Alex anything? What happened? Why did they part?"

"They thought if they split up, one of them could get help."

"How did they get lost?"

"They snuck away from Camp Yukon and were playing in the woods. All I know was a man spooked them."

A man? Were those boot prints they saw *that* man's? If so, the man had not only spooked them but followed them—followed Robbie. What if it was her ex-husband? Could Keith have found them? He'd never cared about his son, but he might kidnap him to get back at her. Her chest suddenly felt constricted. Each breath of air she inhaled burned her throat and lungs.

No. Keith couldn't have found them. *Please, God, it can't be him.* Memories inundated Ella as she fought for a decent breath.

"Ella?" David's concerned voice wrenched her back to the present. "Ella, are you all right?"

No. "We're following Robbie's tracks. We should find him soon." If she said it often enough, it might come true.

"I'll find out more when Travis gets here. I'll call you when I hear something else."

When Ella hung up, she realized she'd slowed her gait to a crawl as she'd talked with David. The space between her and Josiah had doubled. She hurried her pace to catch up with him.

"That was David. Your sister found Travis. That's encouraging." But Robbie and his friend Michael could still be in danger. And there was still a possibility that her ex, Keith, could be the man who had spooked the kids.

"Any info on what happened?" Josiah kept trailing Buddy.

"They were playing in the woods when a man scared them. That's all I know."

Josiah paused and twisted around, his tan face carved in a frown. "I don't see any evidence now that anyone is following Robbie."

"But what about the man? The boot prints we found? He could—"

Suddenly a series of barks echoed through the trees.

"Come on. Buddy has something."

Ella ran beside Josiah, who slowed down to allow her to keep up. Buddy sat at the base of a tree, barking occasionally, looking up, then at them.

"Robbie's up in the tree," Josiah said, slightly ahead of her now.

She examined the green foliage and saw Robbie clinging to a branch. He was safe. *Thank You, Lord. Thank You.*

But what about the man? The threat was still out there. The threat that could be Keith.

As she neared, she noticed her son's wide brown eyes glued to Buddy. The fear on his face pierced through her. He might not recognize the German shepherd. "We're here, Robbie," she shouted. "Buddy is a search and rescue dog. He belongs to Josiah Witherspoon. You remember Mr. Witherspoon?"

Robbie barely moved his head in a nod, but he did look toward her. "Mom, I'm stuck."

Standing under the cottonwood, Ella craned her neck and looked up at him. She wasn't even sure how he'd managed to climb so high. He must be thirty feet off the ground. "Don't do anything yet. You'll be all right. Josiah and I will talk about the best way to get you down safely. Okay?" Her heart clenched at the sight of tears in her son's eyes. His grip around the branch seemed to tighten. He was so scared. All she wanted to do was hold her child and tell him she wouldn't let anything hurt him.

Josiah moved closer. "I can get him down. I have a longer reach than you."

"You don't think he can back down, keeping his arms around the limb?"

"Sometimes people freeze once they get into a tree and see how high they are. I have a feeling he was scared when he climbed up, then realized where he was. I did that once when I was a boy, not much younger than Robbie."

"But should I—"

"You should be a mom and keep him calm."

She nodded, relieved Josiah was here because she was afraid of heights. She would have climbed the tree if she had to, but then there might have been two people stuck up there. "Thanks."

Josiah hoisted himself up onto the lowest branch that would hold his weight, then smiled at her. "I once had a tree where I loved to hide from the world, or rather, Alex when she bugged me. She never knew where I went. I used to watch her try to find me from my perch at the top."

For the first time in hours, Ella chuckled. "I won't tell her, in case you ever want to hide from her again."

He began scaling the branches. "Much appreciated."

"I won't, either," Robbie said in a squeaky voice.

"Thanks, partner," Josiah said to her son, halfway up the main trunk of the cottonwood. "Ella, call David and tell him we found Robbie."

Robbie stared down at the German shepherd. "What's his name?"

While her son talked with Josiah about his dog, Ella gave David a call. "He's in a tree, but Josiah is helping him down. We'll return to base soon." She lowered her voice while she continued. "Has Michael been found yet?"

"No, but I'll pull everyone off the other areas to concentrate on the trail Jesse is following."

"Are the police there?"

"Yes, Thomas Caldwell is here. He's talking with Travis and getting a description of the man."

Thomas was a friend of David's and Josiah's as well as a detective on the Anchorage police force. "Good. We'll be there soon."

When Ella disconnected the call, she watched Josiah shimmy toward Robbie as far as it was safe for him to go on the branch. He was probably one hundred and eighty pounds while her son was forty. Josiah paused about seven feet from Robbie.

"I can't come out any farther, Robbie, but I'm here to grab you as you slide backward toward me. Hug the limb and use one hand to move back to me." Josiah's voice was even and calm, as though they were discussing the weather.

"I can't. I'm...I'm scared. What if I fall?" Robbie peered at the ground and shook his head.

"Don't look down. Do you see that squirrel on the branch near you? He's watching you. Keep an eye on him."

"He's probably wondering what we're doing up here." Robbie stared at the animal, its tail twitching back and forth.

Her son scooted a few inches down the limb, which was at a slight incline from the trunk. When the squirrel scurried away, Robbie squeezed his eyes shut and continued to move at a snail's pace. Finally, when he was within a foot of Josiah, her son raised his head and glanced back at Josiah. His gaze drifted downward, and he wobbled on the branch, sliding to the side.

Ella gasped.

Josiah moved fast, latching on to Robbie's ankle. "I've got you. You're okay."

But her son flailed again. "I'm gonna…"

He fell off the limb, screaming. Then suddenly he was hanging upside down, dangling from the end of Josiah's grip. Robbie's fingertips grazed a smaller branch under him, but it wouldn't hold his weight. Ella's legs went weak, but she remained upright.

"Okay, Robbie?" Josiah adjusted his weight to keep balanced.

"Yes," her son barely said.

"You're safe. Nothing is going to happen to you. Hold still. Can you do that?"

"Yes," Robbie said in a little stronger voice.

"I'm lifting you up to me, then we'll climb down together."

Josiah's gaze connected to Ella's, and she had no doubt her son would be safely on the ground in a few minutes. She sank against the tree trunk, its rough bark scraping her arm. She hardly noticed it, though, as Josiah grabbed her son with both hands and brought Robbie to him, the muscles in his arms bunching with the strain.

When Robbie was in the crook of the tree between the trunk and limb, he hugged Josiah. Surprise flitted across the man's face.

He patted her son on the back several times. "Let's get down from here. I don't know about you, but I'm starving for a hamburger and fries."

"Yeah!" Robbie's face brightened with a big grin.

With Josiah's help, her son finally made it to the ground. Robbie threw his arms around Ella, who never wanted to let him go. She kissed the top of his head as he finally wiggled free.

"Can we go eat a burger with Mr. Witherspoon? Can we?"

The eagerness in his voice made it hard to say no, but it wasn't fair to keep Josiah any longer than necessary. "I'm sure he's—"

"I think that's a great idea, Robbie. There's a place not too far from here that's a favorite of mine. After we eat, then I can take you two to the hangar so your mom can pick up her car."

Robbie looked at Buddy. "What about him?"

"He'll be fine while we're inside. I imagine he's pretty tired. He's been working a lot today."

So have you, Ella thought, glimpsing in Josiah the same weariness she felt, but he must have sensed how important doing something normal and nonthreatening was for her son. Usually when Josiah came to a SAR operation, he did his job and went home. He was all business. But not now. The smile he sent her son made her want to join in.

"Can I pet Buddy?" her son asked.

"Sure. He loves the attention." Josiah squatted next to Robbie after he moved to the German shepherd.

"I wish I had a dog like this. No one would bother me."

Josiah peered up at Ella. "You don't need to worry about that man now."

"You know about the man?" Robbie's forehead scrunched.

"Yes." Ella clasped Robbie's shoulder. "Honey, when we get back to camp, you can tell the police what the man looked like. They'll find him."

Robbie ran his hand down Buddy's back, stroking the dog over and over while Josiah stood next to her son. "How's Travis and Michael?"

"Travis is at the command center. They're still looking for Michael. He may even be with Travis by the time we arrive at camp." At least she hoped that was the case. The idea that Michael might still be lost while the man hadn't been found gave her shivers. She rubbed her hands up and down her arms.

The realization it could still be her ex-husband mocked her. Until she found out for certain, she needed to start making plans to leave Anchorage. She'd disappeared once before. She could again. But the thought of leaving the life she had carved out for her and her son in Alaska swelled her throat with emotions she tried not to feel. She loved Anchorage and the people she'd become friends with. She didn't want to leave.

"Let's go. I imagine you've got a camp full of people anxiously waiting to see you." Josiah rose and said to Robbie, "You want to hold Buddy's leash and lead the way?"

Her son's smile grew even more. "Yeah."

Ella fell into step with Josiah while her son took off with Buddy. "Maybe I should think about getting a pet for Robbie."

"I can help you with that. Buddy became a daddy eight weeks ago. My friend will be selling most of the puppies soon, but I can have the pick of the litter free. I hadn't intended to get another dog, so if Robbie wants one, he can have my free one."

"A mix breed or a German shepherd?"

"A purebred German shepherd. This guy trains dogs for search and rescue. He'll keep two pups to train, then sell them later."

Her pride nudged forward. Ever since escaping her abusive marriage in Georgia and relocating to Anchorage, she hadn't depended on others to help her. It had taken all her courage to seek aid through the New Life Organization and break free of Keith. She was thankful to the Lord that she and Robbie had been able to make it on their own without constantly glancing over their shoulders, looking for Keith, who should have been in prison for years. For four years, she'd been able to live without being scared for her life and now... "I can't accept one. You should take the puppy and sell it."

"I don't need the money. Outdoor Alaska is a successful business. I'd much rather see a child happy with a new pet. I always had one while growing up, and they were important to me."

What if it really was Keith in the woods? A dog would only complicate their lives if they had to move. "I appreciate the offer."

He tilted his head, his gaze slanting down at her. "But?"

Her gaze drifted to Robbie with Buddy. "A German shepherd is a big dog. He'll need to be trained. Any suggestions?"

"I can help when the puppy's old enough."

Again the words *I can't accept* perched on the tip of her tongue, but one look at her son petting Buddy shut that impulse down. Her son was frightened more than most children because of the memories of his abusive father and his temper, all directed at her. Although he'd only been four when she'd finally successfully escaped Keith, a raised voice still shook Robbie, and any man with curly blond hair like his father's scared him to the point that he tried to hide if he could.

She didn't realize she'd stopped walking until Josiah's worried voice said, "Are you all right?"

She blinked, noting her son had paused by a big tree and waited for them to catch up. "Thanks for the offer to help train the dog when we get it." She hoped by the time the puppy was old enough to be separated from its mother, she'd know for sure who the man in the woods was.

The corners of his eyes crinkled as he grinned. "Good. My sister has been teasing me lately. Accusing me of being a hermit when I'm not working."

"When did you leave the Marines?"

"Eighteen months ago. Alex and I grew up in Anchorage. We both left, but she came back when our parents died in a small plane crash and took over the running of the family business, Outdoor Alaska."

"Your store has really grown since I first arrived."

"That's all my sister. She's driven."

"And you aren't?" She started walking again, the darkness of the woods throwing Josiah's face in shadows.

"*Driven?* I'm not sure I would use that word to describe me."

"What word *would* you use to describe yourself, then?"

"I'm just not as driven or singularly focused as I once was. Except when searching for a lost person—when someone else's life is in the balance."

What was he not telling her? Studying his closed expression, she knew there was so much more he kept to himself—like she did. She couldn't share her past with anyone. That would put her and her son in danger. What happened today had ended well for Robbie, but if Keith ever found them, she knew it wouldn't. The thought sent a shudder down her spine.

When they arrived at the camp, Robbie saw Travis and ran toward him with Buddy trotting alongside.

Ella scanned the area and glimpsed Detective Thomas Caldwell talking with David. "I hope Michael was found," she said to Josiah.

"I'll get Robbie and Buddy and be right there," Josiah said, and then headed toward the two boys, who stood near a couple of camp counselors and Travis's parents.

Both Thomas and David were frowning. That didn't bode well for Michael. Ella's chest constricted at the thought of the boy still out there. Not far from David stood his wife with Michael's mother. Tears ran down the young woman's face while Bree consoled her.

When Ella joined David and Thomas, she asked in a low voice, "Has Michael been found yet?"

David's mouth lifted in a grin. "Yes, just two minutes ago. He hurt himself. Jesse thinks it's a sprained ankle. He's bringing him in."

"Thank God he's safe. Good thing Bree is here. She can check him on-site." Ella spied her son and Josiah making their way toward her.

David peered at his wife with love deep in his eyes.

David had been fortunate last winter to rescue Bree, a doctor who flew to remote villages, from a downed bush plane in the wilderness. That had been the beginning of a beautiful relationship, which had just culminated in their wedding on Valentine's Day. Sometimes Ella wished she had a special man in her life again, but her marriage to Keith had soured her on marriage. But David deserved some happiness.

How about you? a little voice in her head said.

She was happy. She had her son, friends, a good church and a fulfilling job. She didn't need a man to be happy. And yet, when she saw other married couples who obviously loved each other, a twinge stabbed her with the idea of what could have been if she hadn't married Keith.

"Travis's dad told me Michael has been found," Josiah said.

"Yeah, Mom. Can we wait until he arrives before going to dinner?"

Ella slid a look to Josiah, and he answered her son, "Yes, of course."

"Good. Travis is staying, too. I'm gonna sit with him until Michael shows up."

"Ella, I'd like to ask Robbie a few questions," Thomas said.

"Yes, of course."

Thomas smiled at her son. "It's nice to see you again. That picnic David threw on the Fourth of July was great. We'll need to work on him to have one for Labor Day, especially if his father is going to be the chef."

"Yeah. My favorite part was the fireworks." Still clutching Buddy's leash, Robbie stroked the German shepherd as he craned his neck to peer up at Thomas.

"Travis told me what happened, but I'd love to hear it from you, too."

The grin on her son's face vanished. "We were over there." Robbie gestured toward the line of trees near the camp base. "We heard an owl but couldn't see it so we thought we would try to find it." He swung his attention to Ella. "I know we shouldn't have gone away from the camp, but I love birds. I saw a bald eagle earlier today."

"We'll talk about that later. Right now, just tell the detective what you remember."

Pausing for a moment, Robbie tilted his head. "Mom, I think I need to learn how to track. That way I would have known how to get back to camp. We walked for a while, listening to the owl hoot." He closed his eyes for a few seconds, balling his hands. "When I saw a man with a mean face standing by a tree staring at us, I looked around. None of us could really tell which way we'd come from. We were talking and not paying attention. I was gonna inspect the ground for footprints, but the man started heading for us. We ran. Me and Michael followed Travis, thinking he must know the way. He didn't."

"I understand you all split up. Why?" Thomas asked.

"Because the man was still behind us. I've seen it on a TV show. People split up when they are being chased. That way one of us could run back and get help."

"What happened when you did that?" Thomas asked.

"At first, he went after me, but then suddenly he turned and started in the direction Michael went. I decided to climb a tree, but the first one wasn't good. The second one was better." He dropped his head. "Except I couldn't get down. Then Josiah saved me." Robbie's gaze fixed on Josiah.

"What did the man look like?" Thomas wrote on his pad.

"A grizzly bear."

"Robbie, no kidding around. This is serious," Ella scolded him.

"Mom, I know. He was *huge*—" Robbie's arms spread out to indicate not only tall but wide "—and had so much dark brown hair all over him. When I was running and looked back, that was what he reminded me of." Her son trembled. "I don't ever want to see him again. I promise, Mom, I won't ever go off like that."

Relieved that the description didn't fit her ex-husband at all, especially all that dark hair, she released a slow breath. "I'm glad you learned a good lesson." Ella patted his shoulder, realizing the fear Robbie had experienced would be more effective than if she grounded him for a week.

"Anything else about the man that might help me find him?" Thomas scribbled a few more notes on his pad.

Robbie stared at the ground, then slowly shook his

head. "Nope. I was running most of the time. I didn't want him to catch me."

"Thanks, Robbie, for helping me. You can go sit with Travis if you want now." While her son handed Buddy's leash to Josiah then left, Thomas gave Ella his card. "Call me if he remembers anything else. I've got police combing the woods right now. Hopefully we'll find the man. We'll work on a composite sketch after I talk with Michael. I'd like to show the boys the picture our artist comes up with and see what they think. Okay?"

"Yes. I want him found. I don't like the idea someone is out there chasing children."

"Neither do I. My partner is checking the database of criminals who target children in Anchorage to see if one matches the description."

The realization of how close Robbie had come to being taken by a stranger finally took hold of Ella. The campsite spun before her eyes while her legs gave way.

THREE

As Ella began to sink to the ground, Josiah grabbed her and held her up. "When was the last time you ate something?" He looked into her eyes, making sure she hadn't fainted.

"I don't remember," she answered with a shaky laugh. "I was so worried about Robbie, I wasn't thinking about eating."

"Let's go sit on the bench over there." Josiah's arm held her protectively against his side, and he moved toward the wooden seat off to the side.

"Thanks." Ella closed her eyes and breathed deeply.

When David approached, he said, "I'll get something to hold you over until you can eat a real meal." He left for a moment and was back with a granola bar and a bottle of water. "Sorry it's not more, but this should tide you over for the time being."

She took a bite of the granola bar and took a sip of water. "I started thinking about what could have happened if that man had caught Robbie or one of the other boys."

"But he didn't. Keep your focus on that. What-ifs don't matter." The feel of her close to him accelerated his heart rate as if he were running with Buddy. He gently eased her onto the wooden bench, then sat next to her, worried about her pale features.

She dropped her head, her chin nearly touching her chest. Her long blond hair fell forward, hiding her delicate features. What had drawn him to her from the beginning, when he'd met her months ago, were her large brown eyes. One look into them and he'd experienced a kinship with her, as if she'd gone through a nightmare that equaled his. He hoped he was wrong, because being a prisoner of war was intolerable, even for the strongest person.

"Robbie is all I have. I can't let anything happen to him. That man could have hurt him today." Ella finished the granola bar and gulped down some water.

"He could have, but he didn't. The boy is safe. The police will find the man who chased the kids. If he has any kind of record, it'll only be a matter of time before he's found and arrested."

She angled her head to look into his eyes. For a few seconds everything around him faded. His focus homed in on her face. When she smiled, her whole face lit up, and for a moment, he thought he was special to her. Why in the world would he think that? For the past eighteen months, he'd slowly been piecing his life back together, but at the moment he felt as if all he'd been able to do was patch over the wounds.

"Thanks, Josiah. You've gone above and beyond for me. Neither of us got much sleep last night because of Mr. Otterman's search, but I wasn't following a dog on a scent. You were. I hate to impose on you about dinner—"

He covered her hand with his. "I usually have dinner alone after a long day at Outdoor Alaska. Going out with you and your son will be a nice change of pace. Besides, Robbie is expecting me to go. I don't want to let him down. And you are *not* imposing on me."

For the past six months, since returning to Alaska, he'd gone through the same routine every day—wake up, grab breakfast on the run, work long hours at the store, then go home, eat dinner, play with Buddy and then go to bed. Not much else in between. The only time he deviated from the schedule was when he and Buddy helped in a search and rescue. His volunteering had been a lifesaver for him.

Dimples appeared on her cheeks. "All right, then. Dinner it is. And there's more to life than work, you know. I would have thought you would enjoy camping at this time of year."

For a second, all he could do was stare at her smile until he realized she was waiting for him to say something. "I used to camp a lot, but since I left the Marines, I haven't."

"Alaska is a great place to enjoy the outdoors, even in the winter. That's what I love about this state."

"I know what you mean." He wanted to steer the conversation away from him. He glimpsed fellow searcher Jesse coming out of the trees, carrying a boy. Jesse's dog trotted next to him. "There's Jesse and Michael." He pointed in their direction.

Before Ella could say anything, Robbie and Travis raced toward them. "Well, I guess I don't have to tell my son Michael is back."

"We'll give him a few minutes to talk with his friend, then leave. I've worked up quite an appetite."

"It's all that exercising you did today."

"You were right there by my side, looking for Robbie. You must be hungry, too." Josiah rose and offered his hand.

She took it and stood. "Thanks for all your help." When Michael was taken to the first-aid tent, Ella motioned to Robbie to join her.

Her son skidded to a stop. "Let's go. I could eat a bear." Suddenly he swung his head from side to side. "No one has seen a bear, have they?"

"No."

"Good. I really can't eat a bear, but I'm so hungry."

"Then let's go." Josiah indicated where his truck was parked. "Would you like to take Buddy, Robbie?"

"Sure!"

"I need to talk to the camp director first," Ella said, approaching the man.

Josiah watched Ella talk with the guy. From her body language, he could guess what she was saying to the director. It was clear she wasn't happy with what happened today, and Josiah couldn't blame her. She was more restrained than he would have been if Robbie were his son. At one time he'd envisioned having a family, but not after his fiancée, Lori's, betrayal. The thought of her had been what kept him going while he'd been a prisoner of war, but when he'd escaped his three-month captivity, she'd already moved on with her life with another man.

When Ella returned, her expression was blank except for a glint in her brown eyes. "Okay, I'm ready."

"I need to see Thomas for a second." He gave Ella his truck keys. "Go on. I'll be there shortly."

Josiah jogged toward the tent and waited in the

entrance while Thomas finished interviewing Michael. He caught the detective's attention, and Thomas walked to him. "I know you're going to let Ella know your progress in finding the man who scared the boys, but I'd appreciate it if you'd call me first."

Thomas's eyebrows shot up. "I didn't realize you two were so close."

"We aren't. Not exactly. But she's a single mother. I don't want her to feel she's all alone in this."

"She isn't. David and Bree asked me to do the same thing." He tried to maintain a tough expression, but his mouth twisted in a slight smile.

Exasperated at Thomas, who he'd known since childhood, Josiah asked, "Does that mean you'll call me first?"

"Yes. Count this as me informing you before Ella. One of my officers at the station just called me. He found a match in the database from the description Travis and Robbie gave me, and I showed Michael the guy's photo. He positively ID'd the guy, so I sent some patrol cars to the last known address of Casey Foster to bring him in for questioning."

"It's probably too much to ask that he'll be home."

"Many criminals do dumb things and get caught." Thomas looked toward Josiah's truck. "I see Ella and Robbie waiting for you."

"Yeah, we're going to grab dinner." Josiah looked up at the clouds as drops of rain began to fall.

"Go on. I'll show Travis the guy's photo. I won't show Robbie until later. I know what a long day you and Ella had, with the earlier search for Mr. Otterman."

"See you later." Josiah turned to leave and nearly

collided with his twin sister. They had similar coloring—black hair, blue eyes—but that was as close as they got to being alike. He and Alex were polar opposites in many respects. They were close, though. She was all the family he had left.

"Just got back from helping to search for Michael. I saw Ella and her son in your truck. Is Robbie okay?"

"Shook up but not hurt."

"Travis, too. But I understand Michael sprained his ankle."

"He hurt it while running, I hear."

"At least this one ended well. It's been a good day for us. Will you be home for dinner?"

Alex lived in their large family house with a housekeeper and caretaker while he stayed in a small cabin behind his childhood home. He would sometimes eat dinner with his sister and discuss business. The place was really too big even for the both of them, but they hadn't wanted to sell the house they'd grown up in after their parents died, which was one of the reasons he'd wanted to be involved in search and rescue. It had been the cold, not the plane crash, that had killed them before they could be found. "No, I'm taking Ella and Robbie for a hamburger at Stella's Café."

"I love Stella's. I'd join you, but I'm half-asleep right now."

"See you later, sis." His stomach rumbling, he quickened his pace.

The sight of Ella looking out his windshield—as if she belonged there—spurred his pulse rate. He'd avoided getting too close to others since he'd come home, except for a few he'd known all his life like Thomas, Jesse and his sister. But even with them, he couldn't reveal the horrors he'd endured. His body had healed, but his heart still felt ripped in two. He'd closed part of himself off in order to survive for those three months as a captive.

He climbed into his cab and twisted around to look at Robbie. "You okay back there with Buddy?"

The boy smiled from ear to ear. "Yup."

Josiah started his truck just as the forecasted rain finally started falling. Twenty minutes later, when he pulled into the parking lot of Stella's Café, the small storm was already clearing up. When he switched off his engine, he looked at Ella, her head leaning against the window, her eyes closed. Then he peered in the backseat. Robbie, curled against Buddy, slept, too. He hated to wake them up. But before he could do anything, his dog lifted his head and barked a couple of times.

Ella shot up straight in her seat while Robbie groaned, laid his hand on Buddy and petted him. The sight of both of them shifted something deep inside Josiah.

"That wasn't exactly how I planned to wake you up, but it was effective."

Ella laughed. "That it was."

Robbie stretched and pushed himself up to a sitting position, rubbing his eyes. "We're here?"

"Yes, but if you two want, I can get it to go."

Ella shook her head. "No, burgers are best eaten right away, especially the fries."

Within five minutes, Robbie sat across from Josiah while Ella was in the seat next to him.

Robbie glanced around, his eyes lighting up when

he saw a couple of video games lining one wall. "Can I play?"

"Just until our food arrives." Ella dug into her purse and gave her son some quarters.

When he left, Josiah knew this might be the only time Robbie wasn't around to hear the news Thomas had told him about Casey Foster. Dread twisted his gut just thinking Foster had been in the park near the boys. "Thomas has a lead on a man he suspects scared the children."

She clasped her hands tightly together on the table. "Someone with a record?"

"Yes. His name is Casey Foster. The police have been sent to pick him up. Michael identified a photo Thomas showed him."

"Good. I don't want him frightening any other children at the camp."

"Speaking of the camp, how did it go with the director?" The second the question was out of his mouth, he wanted to snatch it back. He didn't usually pry into other people's lives, especially someone who was an acquaintance—well, a little more than an acquaintance, especially after today. Search and rescue operations tended to bring people closer. But when that happened, he felt too vulnerable and often needed to step away.

"I'm pulling Robbie out of the camp. It's no longer a safe environment. Mr. Waters assured me the counselor who failed to watch the boys would be fired, but I can't take that chance again. Of course, I'm going to have to find other arrangements for Robbie until school starts. I'll talk with David tomorrow. I might have to take a few days off while I look."

"That camp has a good reputation."

"I know. I wanted Robbie to learn about Alaska, some survival tips and how to take care of himself. It was a bonus that a couple of his friends were going to the camp, too. I'll call Michael's and Travis's parents to see what they're going to do. Child care is a big issue, especially when I don't have any family here."

"Where are you from?"

Ella averted her gaze for a few seconds before answering, "Back east."

A shutter fell over her expression, and her eyes darkened. He could tell when someone didn't want to continue a thread of conversation, and he was definitely getting vibes on that score. What was she hiding? The question aroused his curiosity, which wasn't a good thing. He needed to step away before she became more than a casual friend, someone he worked with from time to time.

Ella stood. "I see the waitress coming. I'm going to get Robbie."

The older lady placed their burgers and fries on the table as Robbie hurried back to his seat.

"This smells great." The young boy popped a fry into his mouth.

"Where's your mom?"

"She went to the restroom."

As though she needed to step back. *Interesting.* More and more Ella reminded him of himself. He knew why he was reluctant to become emotionally close to a person. What was her reason?

"How long have you had Buddy?" Robbie asked before taking a big bite of his burger.

"Eighteen months, since I left the Marines." Buddy

had entered his life as a service dog because he'd been diagnosed with post-traumatic stress disorder. Out of the corner of his eye, Josiah caught sight of Ella returning to the table.

"How long has Buddy been a search and rescue dog?"

"I started training Buddy a year ago." Buddy had helped him so much, Josiah wanted to help others with his German shepherd.

Ella slipped into her chair, her expression closed. "Is the burger good?" she asked her son.

"Great. Mr. Witherspoon did good choosing this place. We need to come back here."

"Call me Josiah. Mr. Witherspoon makes me sound old."

Finally she looked at him. Again he couldn't tell what she was thinking.

"Is that okay with you?" Josiah drenched his fries with ketchup.

She nodded, then began eating. If it hadn't been for Robbie, the tension at the table could have been cut with a hunting knife. More questions filled Josiah's mind. Did this have to do with the reason she was a single parent? A bad marriage? Did her husband die?

Stop! Don't go there.

"Who was the first person you rescued?" Robbie asked, pulling Josiah away from his thoughts about Ella.

"It was a couple who got lost in Denali National Park." Josiah went on to tell the boy about how Buddy had located them.

By the time the meal was over, Ella's stiff posture

had finally relaxed. "I know David appreciates all the time you and your sister give to the organization."

"Alex and I have some freedom in our work because we own the business. We can often leave at a moment's notice. I know others like Jesse can't because he works as a K-9 officer for the Anchorage Police."

His plate empty, Robbie sat back, yawning.

Ella chuckled. "I think that's our cue to go home. It has been a *long* day."

Josiah laid money on the bill the waitress had left and rose. "Let's go. I need to see if David is at the office. We still need to discuss Saturday's training."

"I forgot all about that." Ella made her way to the exit. "Robbie, I guess you'll be going to work with me tomorrow."

Robbie perked up. "I will? Neat."

"I think you'll find the everyday operations of the Northern Frontier Search and Rescue are boring," Ella said when they were back in the truck.

Robbie sat next to Buddy. The dog opened his eyes to note who was in the cab, then went back to sleep. "Buddy has the right idea." He yawned again.

Ella looked sideways at Josiah. "He'll probably fall asleep on the way home. I would, too, but since I'm driving, I can't."

"I can take you two home and even pick you up and take you to work tomorrow, if you'd like. I wouldn't want you to fall asleep at the wheel."

"No, I'm fine. I'm tired but not that sleepy."

At Northern Frontier's hangar, where the organization's office was located, Josiah parked next to Ella's Jeep at the side of the building. While she and Robbie climbed into her car, he headed into the open hangar since he saw David's SUV inside it.

David emerged from the office and halted when he spied Josiah. "Thanks for the help today."

"I'm glad both situations ended well. I just brought Ella back to pick up her car. She's taking Robbie home right now."

"After you all left the park, Thomas received a report that another boy went missing nearby in a residential area."

"Taken by this Casey Foster?" Anger festered in Josiah. What if he hadn't found Robbie?

"Don't know yet. Thomas promised to let me know. It may turn out to be nothing."

"Let's hope. When he calls, make sure he keeps me informed. Is there going to be a search?"

"Maybe. I won't know until Thomas assesses the situation. If there's reason to believe foul play, the police may use their K-9 unit and not need any extra help."

"I know it's hard to think about this on top of all that's happened, but what about the training on Saturday? That's why I came in here, to see when you and I can meet about it."

"I don't know how effective I would be right now. Let's meet tomorrow morning, say eleven?"

"Sounds good." Weariness finally began to set in as Josiah returned to his truck to drive home.

As he left the airport, his cell rang. When he realized it was Thomas, he pulled to the side of the road to take the call. "David told me there's another boy missing."

"No, he was found, but he ran from a man in a vehicle, who was trying to get him into it. The car had been reported stolen earlier—guess where from? An address a few houses down from where Casey Foster lives. I'm at Foster's house right now. He's not here. I have a BOLO out on him and the car. We'll stake this place out and see if he turns up."

"Have you called Ella yet?"

"No, but I feel like she needs to know Foster hasn't been found."

"I'll swing by her place and tell her. I'd hate for her to hear this over the phone."

"Are you sure? This has been an extralong day for you." There was a hint of curiosity in his friend's voice.

Josiah could imagine the grin on Thomas's face. He and Jesse were longtime friends who knew about his ex-fiancée. Thomas had even tried to fix him up on a date when he had returned to Anchorage. Josiah had declined the offer. "Yes. I want to make sure Robbie is okay."

"Sure. See you at Saturday's training."

If not before hung in the air for a few seconds before Josiah said goodbye and disconnected the call.

Fifteen minutes later he arrived at Ella's house and walked up to her porch with Buddy. If Robbie was still awake, he'd want to see his dog. Before he pushed the doorbell, he steeled himself. He hated telling Ella that the police hadn't found Foster yet, but she needed to know.

When she appeared at the front door, he smiled at the sight of her. She was a beautiful woman who cared about people. And he wanted to know who or what had put that sadness in her eyes.

"Josiah? What brings you by?"

"I heard from Thomas."

"Come in." After she closed the door, she swept her arm toward the living room. "I have a feeling I need to sit down to hear what you have to say."

What was he doing here? Why did he feel he needed to be the one to talk to her? Josiah cleared his throat and proceeded to impart the news concerning the attempt on another boy and the disappearance of Foster.

The color drained from Ella's face. "So he's out there looking for his next victim."

"Everyone is searching for him."

"Then I'll pray the police find him soon before another child is terrorized."

"Where's Robbie?" Josiah sat across from Ella with Buddy at his feet.

"He went right to bed. Fell asleep on the ride home from the airport."

"Good. He needs the rest."

Buddy rose and began growling. Josiah bolted to his feet at the same time Ella did.

She opened her mouth to say something, but a scream reverberated from the back of the house. "It's Robbie."

FOUR

Ella froze at the sound of her son's scream. Josiah and Buddy charged toward the living room doorway. Ella raced after them, overtaking them in the hallway.

"This way." Ella told them, hoping it was only a nightmare caused by today's events.

"Mom! Mom!" Robbie yelled, flying out of his bedroom at the end of the hall.

But the fright on his face belied that hope. He pointed a shaking hand toward his doorway, his eyes wide with fear. "He's...outside my...my window." Robbie swung his attention from her to Josiah then Buddy.

As Ella knelt in front of Robbie and clasped his arms, Josiah said, "I'll take a look outside."

"Use the back door in the kitchen." Ella kept her focus on her son while the sound of Josiah's footsteps faded. "Tell me what happened, honey."

"I woke up. Don't know why. When I sat up, I looked out the window." In the entrance to his bedroom, Robbie lifted his arm and pointed at the closed window at the end of his bed. "I saw..." Robbie began to tremble.

Ella hugged her son as though she could protect him from anything. She wished. "What did you see, honey?"

Robbie hiccupped, then said, "A man staring at me."

Chills flashed through Ella, her heartbeat thumping against her chest like a ticking bomb. "Did you know the man?"

"I don't know. Maybe the guy at the park. It all happened so fast. When I yelled, he ran away."

"Josiah and Buddy will check it out. I see them outside right now." She crossed to the window, watching while Buddy sniffed the ground before she closed the blinds. Her son liked to fall asleep in the summer with the blinds open since he was scared of the dark. From now on, he would have to be satisfied with a night-light. "No one can see you now. You're safe."

Standing in the entrance, Robbie clutched the door frame. "I don't feel safe."

"Tell you what. Why don't you camp out in the living room?"

"By myself?"

Ella pulled the navy blue comforter and pillow off his bed. "There's no way I'm gonna let you have all the fun. I'm camping out, too."

"Can we ask Josiah and Buddy to stay?"

Before today, the question would have been totally rejected. But after everything that had happened, the thought of being alone made her afraid.

Under Robbie's window, Buddy caught a scent and tugged on his leash. Josiah followed him around the side of Ella's house and across the front yard into the street. Buddy headed to the left along the curb past three of Ella's neighbors before his dog stopped and sniffed the road. Buddy stared at Josiah and barked.

He petted Buddy. "It looks like the person left in a car. At least we know he's gone."

He prayed that was the case, but as Josiah walked back to Ella's, his concern for her and Robbie grew. What if it was Foster, and he'd snatched the boy? After what happened earlier today, he would have thought the man would lose himself in the wilderness north of Anchorage rather than stick around and go after one of the kids he'd harassed in the park.

He retrieved his cell phone from his pocket and called Thomas. When his friend came on the line, Josiah said, "I came over to Ella's house to let her know about Foster, and while I was here, Robbie saw a man outside his bedroom window looking in. Buddy and I checked it out and Buddy trailed the scent down the street until it vanished between the third and fourth house to the left of Ella's."

"You think it was Foster and he drove away?"

"Maybe it was Foster. I can't be sure. But how would Foster know where Ella lived?"

"Wish I knew. It could have been someone else, but either way, a man was peeking into Robbie's bedroom. Not good." The controlled anger in Thomas's voice conveyed his concern about the situation. "I'll come out and take a look. Not sure there's much the police can do. I've got everyone out looking for Foster. If he's still in Anchorage, hopefully we'll find him soon. We're notifying the public to be on the lookout. Maybe a citizen will see him and report his location."

Josiah climbed the stairs to Ella's porch. "See you

in a while." After disconnecting, he knocked on Ella's door.

When she let him in a minute later, her arms were
full of bedding. "We're camping out in the living
room and making sure the blinds are pulled tight.
I'm hoping it helps take his mind off the man peeking in the window." She lowered her voice and asked,
"Did you find anything?"

He nodded. "I called Thomas. He's on the way."

Ella pressed her lips together, walked into the living room and set the covers on the floor. "I was hoping he was wrong."

"Where's Robbie?"

"The bathroom. He'll be here in a minute."

Josiah quickly told Ella what he and Buddy found,
the whole time keeping an eye on the hallway. He
didn't want to upset Robbie any more than he already
was.

She sighed. "I know Thomas will want to talk
to Robbie, but can you explain and show Thomas
the window? I don't want Robbie traumatized any
more than he already is. My son doesn't know who
it was for sure. If he remembers something, I'll call
Thomas."

"I'll take care of it. There might not be much he
can do, but I wanted Thomas to know about it. When
he comes, I'll talk with him out on the porch."

"I've decided it's time we get a dog. Is the offer
still good for one of Buddy's puppies?"

"Yes, but it'll be a while before the puppy could
be a watchdog."

Ella edged closer, glancing back at the hallway.

"Just having a dog in the house would make my son feel safer." Her gaze locked with his. "Me, too."

"Then I'll talk to the breeder and see about arranging a time to see the puppies. Robbie can pick out one, and when the breeder thinks he's ready to come home with you, I can start working with you and Robbie. That is, if you want me to."

A smile spread across her face. "I was hoping you'd say that."

His pulse kicked up a notch. "I said I would, and when I make a promise, I keep it." Josiah caught sight of Robbie coming toward them and turned toward the boy. "I hear you and your mom are going to have a campout in the living room. You could even make a fire in the fireplace and roast marshmallows."

Robbie's eyes grew round. "Mom, can we?"

"Only if Josiah goes out and gets the firewood," she said with a chuckle.

"Will you? We could make s'mores. Isn't that right, Mom?"

"I think I have everything we need."

Josiah remembered having s'mores as a child. He once ate so many he got sick, but that didn't stop him from loving them. "Sounds good to me. Just point me in the right direction."

"On the right side of the house by the garage."

Seconds later the doorbell rang.

"Do you want me to get it?" Josiah watched Ella struggle to contain her concern. He tried to imagine what she was going through. To have a child threatened or hurt had to be a parent's worst nightmare.

"Yes. Robbie and I will be checking to make sure we have enough of everything for the s'mores."

"I'll leave Buddy with you two." Josiah passed the leash to the boy. "You're in charge of him."

"Sure thing. I'll take good care of him. I promise." Robbie petted the top of Buddy's head.

The chimes sounded again.

"I'd better get the door." Josiah walked toward the foyer.

"And we gotta get some wire coat hangers," Robbie said as he and Ella headed to the kitchen.

Josiah waited until they disappeared before he opened the front door. He walked out on the porch to talk with Thomas.

Thomas frowned. "I was beginning to wonder if something else had happened."

"Sorry about that. Ella didn't want Robbie to know you were here. She asked me to talk to you and show you where the guy was."

"But I need to talk with Robbie."

"Can you wait until tomorrow? The kid is pretty shook up, and she's trying to divert his attention from the day's incidents." Josiah descended the steps.

Still on the porch, Thomas nodded. "I understand. I'll take some pictures and check for latent prints on the windowsill. Did Robbie tell you anything about the man?"

"No, he didn't. He might remember something later." Josiah rounded the back of the house and stopped near Robbie's bedroom window. "This is one of those times when I'm glad it's light out till ten-thirty at night."

Thomas took photos of the boot prints in the dirt and then dusted for fingerprints on the ledge. "You didn't touch any of this?"

"No. I think the boot print looks similar in size to the one I followed earlier today in the woods."

Thomas turned toward Josiah. "Let's hope one of these prints on the sill is in the system."

"Will you let me know before you call Ella? If it's Foster, that means the man discovered where Robbie lives and came after him."

Thomas's forehead wrinkled. "You think he targeted Robbie in the woods?"

"Not exactly, but maybe he's fixated on the boys. After all, they got away from him."

"I'll talk with the parents of the two other boys and alert them, especially if one of these prints ends up being Foster's."

Josiah started for the right side of the house. "Good. I'm going to stay the night. I'd never get any sleep if I left them unprotected."

Thomas grinned. "Does Ella know you're staying?"

Josiah shot him an exasperated look as he bent over and lifted several logs. "Not yet. If I have to, I'll guard them from outside."

"This is the first time I've seen you so invested in a search and rescue case."

"Ella is a friend, and she's alone with an eight-year-old. If you were me, you wouldn't walk away, either." Josiah started for the front of the house.

"No, I wouldn't. I'm glad to see your interest. Since you returned home, you haven't gotten involved in much other than work and volunteering for Northern Frontier. Jesse and I have to practically kidnap you to get you to do anything else."

"Most of my spare time has gone to training Buddy."

Thomas stopped at the bottom of the porch. "Your dog is trained better than most. I think you can relax and enjoy yourself from time to time."

Josiah glanced at his childhood friend. "Look who's talking. When was the last time *you* went out on a date?"

"Okay. I know work has demanded more of my time lately, so maybe when things settle down you, Jess and I can go camping before winter sets in."

"Sounds good. See you." While Thomas headed for his car, Josiah scanned the neighborhood. Everything appeared peaceful, but as he knew firsthand, that could change in an instant.

He entered Ella's house with the logs, locked the front door and made his way to the fireplace. Robbie, Buddy and Ella came into the living room as he stacked the wood for a fire.

"Do you want me to start it now?" When Josiah peered over his shoulder at Ella, he caught her staring at Robbie kneeling next to Buddy and stroking him.

Her gaze shifted toward Josiah, and a blush tinted her cheeks. "I was telling Robbie in the kitchen about getting a puppy soon."

The boy grinned so big, a gap in his upper teeth showed a missing incisor. "Can we go get it tomorrow? I'm ready. See how good I am with Buddy?"

"I'll have to call the breeder and see what day works for him." Josiah finished setting the logs on the grate, started the fire and stood up.

"Robbie, I know you're excited, but I told you it might be a few days. Besides, I'll be tied up tomorrow at work, then Saturday I'll be working at the training session. All day."

"But, Mom, I *need* a dog."

"You don't need a dog. You want one. And I realize that." She faced Josiah. "So we'll be available anytime after Saturday."

"Okay. I'll let you know what I can arrange." The sight of Robbie's shoulder drooping prompted Josiah to add, "I'll be busy with the training session all day Saturday, too."

Robbie opened his mouth to say something, but Ella interrupted. "No arguing."

The boy pouted. "How did you know I was gonna do that?"

She smiled, her brown eyes sparkling. "Let's just say it's a mom thing."

"Did you have all the ingredients for the s'mores?" Josiah asked. "I can fix the hangers if you want."

"Good. I couldn't find my pliers." She gave him the two wire hangers she held. "We have more than enough supplies, except for hangers. It's getting late, Robbie, so I'll let you fix a couple of s'mores but that's all. We have to go to work early tomorrow."

"Can Buddy—" Robbie glanced at Josiah "—and you stay the night? We're camping out in here. It'll be fun." The boy grinned, but the corners of his mouth quivered as though he was forcing the smile. Trying to be brave.

Josiah could remember he'd done the same thing. Putting on a front for everyone around him when things were wrong. "It's your mother's call." He switched his focus to Ella, whose expression was unreadable.

"Robbie, I think we could use something to drink. Get the milk and three glasses, please."

The boy trudged toward the hallway, his shoulders slumped, his head down. At the doorway, he swiveled toward his mother. "Please, Mom. I know you can take care of me, but you're a girl."

Ella gave her son *the look*.

Robbie hurried away.

"What do you want me to do?" Josiah said when the boy disappeared.

"I..." Her chest rose and fell with a deep inhalation and exhalation.

He closed the space between them and almost clasped her upper arms, but stopped himself and left his hands at his sides. "I think I should stay. I'm not comfortable leaving you alone after what happened at the park and then here today. There's safety in numbers." One corner of his mouth tilted, hoping to coax her into a smile.

"Don't feel obligated to stay. I don't want to be..." She swallowed hard.

"What?" This time he did take one of her hands. "If you're going to say a burden, stop right there."

She grinned. "I was going to say a nuisance. Tonight was probably not connected to the park. I know the Millers down the street were robbed last month. Maybe it was someone casing my house."

"That's not a good thing, either. Let me put it this way. I wouldn't sleep at all if you and Robbie were here by yourselves after this scare." He didn't want to tell her he was pretty sure it was Foster outside Robbie's window. The boot print was too similar. "Do me a favor and let me stay. I need some sleep, especially after last night."

She sighed. "Okay."

"Yippee!" came from the direction of the kitchen.

Ella's cheeks flamed. "Quit eavesdropping, Robbie, and bring the drinks." Then to Josiah, she said, "Sorry about that."

She gently tugged her hand from his, and Josiah instantly missed the contact. He was thankful Robbie entered the living room when he did.

While Ella organized the s'mores production, Josiah watched her work with Robbie. Ella was a wonderful mother. He and Alex had had good parents who expressed their love all the time. Their deaths had been hard on them, but he'd grown up thinking one day he would have his own family and be a dad like his. Now he didn't know if he could.

His captors hadn't taken just three months away from him, but much more. They'd left him with deep emotional scars he wasn't sure would ever totally heal. Since he'd come home, he'd had only one episode of anxiety when he'd heard a car backfire. Maybe he wasn't the best person to guard Ella and Robbie, but there wasn't anyone else right now.

Early the next morning while Robbie and Josiah slept in the living room, Ella sat at the kitchen table, sipping coffee. She'd opened the blackout blinds in the alcove and stared outside into the backyard, which afforded her a view of her neighbors' homes on each side and behind her. If she got a dog, she would need to fence off the area. Maybe she needed to reconsider. She didn't have a lot of money to spend on something like that.

And yet, having an animal in the house appealed to her. A dog like Buddy would make her feel safer—

like an alarm system. After the first two years living here in Anchorage, she should have looked into getting a pet. Robbie had wanted one, but she'd still been worried Keith would find them somehow. And having a pet would make fleeing harder.

Yesterday for a short time, that fear had dominated her as she searched for Robbie. She'd actually been thankful it had been Casey Foster. That meant her ex-husband hadn't discovered their whereabouts.

Thank You, Lord. I don't know what I would have done if Keith had been the one in the woods. It was hard enough fleeing him the first time and giving up my friends and family. At least I have You and Robbie.

"You're an early riser," Josiah said from the doorway into the kitchen.

He'd finger combed his hair, and his clothes were rumpled from staying in the sleeping bag that he kept in the storage container in his truck. But the sight of him soothed any anxiety she felt thinking about her ex-husband.

"Want some coffee? I have a full pot." Ella started to rise.

Josiah waved her down. "I can get it. Do you want a refill?"

She looked at her near-empty mug and nodded. After Josiah poured coffee for them both, he returned the pot to the coffeemaker and settled in the chair across from her.

He peered out the window, his hands cradling his mug. "Five in the morning and it looks like eight or nine anywhere else. I'm still getting used to the long days."

"I thought you were from Alaska."

"Sure. That'll give me time to cook breakfast."

While her son and Josiah walked the German shepherd, Ella hurried to her bedroom and changed for work, then returned to start the pancakes. Twenty minutes later, the batter ready, more coffee perking and the orange juice prepared, she made her way toward the porch to see how much longer Robbie and Josiah were going to be. Halfway across the foyer the doorbell rang. Glancing at her watch, she saw it was seven in the morning.

A bit early for visitors, Ella thought as she cautiously peered out the peephole and heaved a sigh of relief. Detective Thomas Caldwell. Then she wondered why he was here so early.

When she swung the door open, she glanced around. "Did you see Josiah and Robbie with Buddy?"

"Yeah, they're heading back here. Josiah got a chance to show me where Buddy lost the scent of the intruder. I thought later I'd check with your neighbors to see if anyone saw a strange car parked there."

She glimpsed Josiah with Robbie and the German shepherd walking across the yard toward the house. "Come in. Would you like to join us for breakfast?"

"Sounds good, but before your son returns, I wanted to let you know about the fingerprints on Robbie's windowsill."

He took a sip of his coffee. "But I was away for years serving in the Marines and got used to more normal days and nights."

"This winter must have been difficult for you, then. I remember that was the harder adjustment for me than the long days."

"The dark doesn't bother me as much as it being light most of the time." Josiah stared at his coffee, and for a long moment silence descended between them.

His thoughtful look made her wonder if he was thinking about something in his past. She'd known he'd served in the Marines in combat situations, but he'd never discussed that time in his life. Then again, she wasn't a close friend.

"I appreciate your staying over. I don't think Robbie would have gone to sleep if you hadn't been here. In fact, I'm not sure I would have, either. Then I'd probably be fired when David found me slumped over the computer keyboard at work later today sound asleep."

Josiah lifted his head, his gaze connecting with hers. "I don't think you have to worry. You've got David wrapped around your finger."

For a few seconds his eyes reflected sadness before he masked it. Again she felt a bond with Josiah, and she wasn't sure why. "I hope so. I'm bringing Robbie to work with me today." She drank several swallows of her coffee. "David is a great boss. He's part of the reason I love my job."

"How did you come to work for Northern Frontier?"

"I was working as a waitress at a café not far from the airport. The man who began and oversaw the search and rescue organization was a frequent customer. He'd come in sometimes, exhausted and frazzled. We started talking, and one thing lead to another. He decided he needed an office manager to run the day-to-day operations of Northern Frontier because of its continual growth."

"I understand David took over Northern Frontier not long before I started volunteering."

"Yes. I've been with the organization for over three years and it has grown in the number of searches we're involved in, as well as in reputation." She loved talking about her work because she felt she was assisting people who needed it.

"My sister had read about Northern Frontier, and when she decided to help, she gave me the idea to volunteer with Buddy, as well."

"Alex has been great to work with. She can rearrange her job to help whenever we need her. You, too."

Josiah grinned. "It helps that we own the business we both work for."

The warmth in his smile enveloped her like an embrace. "Robbie loves Outdoor Alaska. We went to the store right before camp started to get some items he needed. I had a tough time getting him to leave."

"It's more than a store. It's a destination if you're interested in the outdoors, hiking, camping or sports related to Alaska."

"Then what's that mini basketball court doing there?"

"Basketball is alive and well in Alaska. It's a sport that can be played indoors or outdoors. Also, the small court is a great place for kids to pass their time while parents are shopping."

"Who came up with the idea?"

"Me. I like basketball, and sometimes it's a great way to let off steam."

"Must be working. I've never seen you angry. Even in the middle of a crisis, you're calm." Contrary to her ex-husband, who flew off the handle at the slightest provocation, to the point she'd been afraid to say or do anything around him.

"Everyone has a breaking point."

Yes, she of all people knew that. Her limit had been when Keith pushed her down the stairs. Unfortunately, it had been a year after that before she and Robbie could escape him safely.

"Mom. Mom, where are you?" Robbie yelled from the living room.

"I'm in the kitchen." She rose and started for the hallway when her son and Buddy appeared at the other end. "I was about ready to fix us breakfast. Are you up for some blueberry pancakes?"

Robbie's furrowed forehead smoothed out. "Yes." He looked beyond Ella. "Can you and Buddy stay for breakfast? Mom makes the bestest pancakes in the whole state."

"How can I say no to that? I love pancakes and blueberries." Josiah moved closer to Ella. "Is that okay with you?"

She shivered from his nearness. "It's the least I can do after all you've done for me and Robbie."

"Yes!" Robbie pumped his fist in the air. He turned and headed toward the living room, saying, "That means you get to stay, Buddy."

"Can Robbie go with me to walk Buddy? It'll give me a chance to check out your neighborhood."

FIVE

Thomas looked over his shoulder at Robbie and Josiah coming up the steps. The detective quickly whispered, "One set of prints isn't in the system, but the other is Foster's."

"So he found out where Robbie lives." Ella clutched the door frame in the foyer.

Her stomach roiled at the confirmation Foster had been watching her son sleeping last night. A sudden thought blindsided her. She whirled around and raced toward her son's bedroom. She yanked the blackout blind up, then examined the window lock. She sagged against the ledge, gripping the sill as she tried to relax. She couldn't. It was locked. But what if it hadn't been?

The sound of footsteps behind her caused her to turn around. She hoped it wasn't Robbie. Josiah stopped a few feet behind her.

"Thomas told you about Foster being outside the window?"

She nodded and stared out the window at the spot where Foster had stood. "Why has this happened?" *On top of all that I've dealt with in the past, now Foster is after Robbie.*

"Thomas told me he'd do everything he could to find this man. Until then, I'd like you to come stay at my family's home."

She faced him again. "I can't—"

He touched his hand to her cheek, setting her heartbeat racing. "All I ask is that you think about it. I know Alex would love to have you. And Robbie will have two dogs to fall in love with. It would just be until Foster is caught."

Tears clogged her throat. She took in his kind expression, full of compassion. She couldn't remember anyone looking at her quite like that. She swallowed several times before saying, "I'll think about it. I still need to make arrangements for someone to care for Robbie while I work."

"Have you taken any vacation time lately?"

She shook her head.

"Then do. Spend time with Robbie at my family estate. When my sister and I are at work, both Sadie and Buddy stay there along with a couple that take care of the place. Harry is an ex-Marine, and his wife, who is the housekeeper, was a police officer."

"A Marine and a police officer? That's quite a combination. And they're caretakers now?"

"Yup. They've been working for my family for twenty-three years. Harry was my hero growing up. Still is. When he retired after twenty years in the US Marines, he married the love of his life, Linda, and they moved to Alaska. I learned so much of what I know about life and the wilderness from him. My parents were busy people, and Harry and Linda basically raised Alex and me."

"Now I understand why you became a Marine."

"He instilled in me a sense of duty to my country."

"How long did you serve?"

Josiah turned away from her and started for the hallway. "Ten years. You have a lot to do today. We better get moving."

What is he not telling me? She knew when someone was shutting down a conversation. She hated secrets. Keith had always kept a lot of them. She didn't want to go down that road with Josiah, also.

After dropping Ella, Robbie and Buddy off at the Northern Frontier hangar at the small airport, Josiah went to his cabin on the grounds of the estate, showered and changed, then headed for work.

"How's Ella doing after yesterday?" Alex asked Josiah when he entered her office at Outdoor Alaska, on the second floor of the main location.

"Foster came to her house and was peeping into Robbie's room last night. Buddy and I stayed the night with them."

"The police haven't found him yet?"

Josiah settled in the chair in front of his sister's large oak desk, which was neat and organized as usual. "No. Thomas came out to the house and looked around last night, then came back this morning. He showed Robbie some photos, and the kid picked Foster out of the lineup."

Alex scowled. "Eight-year-olds shouldn't have to be doing that."

"That's why I'm here. Ella hasn't said yes yet, but I've invited her and Robbie to stay at the estate. I thought they could stay in the main house with you. If not—"

She waved her hand. "Of course they can. It'll be nice to have a child around, and Sadie will love it."

"Yeah, Buddy has taken to Robbie. I'm going to let them have the pick of the litter."

"Where's Buddy now? Sadie missed her playmate last night."

"I left him with Robbie at the hangar. He promised to walk Buddy and play with him."

"But mostly you want Buddy protecting the boy?"

Josiah nodded. "It's hard for me to comprehend people going after children. I also saw that in the war zone. Too many kids being hurt or killed."

"I don't understand how such evil can exist in this world. Look what happened to you. You were tortured and held captive for months in the Middle East. How could God let that happen when you were saving a group of children from a burning building?"

His sister's faith had been shaky after their parents' deaths, but his captivity had caused her to question even more what the Lord's intentions were. He hated that, and nothing he said would change her mind. "At least the children were saved."

"And I'm glad for that, but you shouldn't have had to pay for it like you did." She pushed to her feet. "Let's just agree to disagree about God. He's constantly letting me down."

"But I'm alive and helping others with Buddy." He'd struggled while a prisoner, but his fiancée and his faith had pulled him through. It was hard enough losing Lori and rebuilding his life because of his capture. He was not going to turn away from the Lord, too.

"Will you still be able to go to the Fairbanks store

and meet with the employees and city officials about the expansion on Monday?"

"Yes."

"What about Robbie and Ella?"

"I might take them with me. A change of scenery could be good for both of them."

One of Alex's eyebrows rose. "First you loan Buddy to them, and now you're including them in your life. Is there more going on than simply protecting the child?"

He frowned. "If I'm protecting them, then I need them close by."

"You haven't been apart from Buddy since you got him."

"I don't need him like I did when I first came back to the States."

"But what if you have an anxiety attack or nightmares?"

"I haven't had one in months, and besides, I have other techniques to help me." Having PTSD after his release from captivity had nearly destroyed him until Buddy had come into his life and he'd gotten help for his panic and anxiety attacks.

"Still, it's good to see you forming friendships outside your small circle of close friends."

"Quit worrying about me, big sis."

"I'm only five minutes older than you, little brother," Alex said with a laugh.

The intercom buzzed, and Alex pressed it down. "Your ten o'clock appointment is here."

"I'm leaving." Josiah stood. "See you tonight."

"Let Linda and Harry know if Ella and Robbie

come to the estate. You know how they are if they don't have any warning."

At the door, Josiah glanced back. "I'm surrounded by organizational freaks. As soon as I know, they'll be informed."

In the reception area, he passed a young gentleman dressed in a three-piece business suit that mocked Josiah's casual clothing of tan slacks and black polo shirt. Later he would load some equipment into his truck to use at tomorrow's training session, but for now he had reports to write on last month's sale numbers.

As he left his sister's office, he again wondered at the differences between Alex and him. She would fit right in with the man who had an appointment, whereas Josiah would be more comfortable in jeans and a T-shirt, but that would shock his sister. If Alex ever saw how messy he was at the cabin, she would be appalled. On second thought, she probably wouldn't be. They knew each other well—in fact, she was the only person who knew how much his captivity had changed him. He hadn't shared that with anyone but Alex and God, and even his sister didn't know all of it.

Ella finished a chart for the training session tomorrow and printed off the copies she would pass out to the participants. Robbie, Buddy and David were out in the hangar setting up some of the areas concerning search and rescue. She checked the wall clock and noted that it was three-thirty. She almost had everything ready to go, then she could go home, get some rest and—

The phone on her desk rang. She snatched up the

receiver. "Northern Frontier Search and Rescue. How can I help you?"

A few seconds' silence, then deep breathing filled the earpiece.

She started to repeat herself when the caller hung up. Ella slowly replaced the phone in its cradle. The second call today. She looked at the caller ID and saw the number was blocked. Since the people who contacted her needed help finding someone, even when she was sure it was a prank call, she stayed on the line in case the person was in trouble.

Was that Foster? If so, why was he calling?

"Mom, what's wrong?" Robbie asked when he came into the office.

"Nothing. Counting down the time until Josiah picks us up."

David appeared in the doorway. "He should be here in an hour with the equipment he's loaning us."

Robbie held on to Buddy's leash. "It's time I take him for a walk. I can do it by myself. I'm only gonna be on the grass near the hangar."

Ella shoved back her chair. "No. I'll come with you. David, I finished the last chart. It's still in the printer. When I get back, I'll put the packets together, and then we should be all ready."

"Great. I want to call it an early evening. Let's pray there aren't any search and rescues tonight or tomorrow." David headed for his office.

"I hope there aren't any the whole weekend. I have some sleep to catch up on." *And how am I going to do that unless I accept Josiah's invitation to stay at his family estate?* He would expect an answer when he came to take her and Robbie home. For the past four years she'd depended only on herself to keep her and Robbie safe. She couldn't tell anyone about her ex-husband. The more people who knew her real past, the greater the risk. The New Life Organization had stressed that to her.

"Mom, Buddy is pacing around. He needs to go outside *bad*." Her son waited by the door that led to the airfield.

"Okay, I'm right behind you."

That was all Robbie needed. He shot out of the office and made a beeline for the patch of grass on the left. At a much more sedate rate Ella followed and gave her son freedom to move in a wide arc with Buddy while she lounged against the building, wondering if it was possible to fall asleep standing up.

Robbie let the dog off the leash to get some exercise. He threw a tennis ball across the grassy area at the side of the hangar to the other end. Buddy barked and raced after it.

Behind Robbie there was a road that was only a few yards from the main street. A black truck, going five or ten miles over the posted speed limit, headed out of the airport. Suddenly the driver swerved the pickup onto the grass, going straight for her son.

"Robbie!" Ella screamed, sprinting as fast as she could toward him. "Run."

Eyes big, Robbie pumped his short legs as fast as she'd ever seen him do. Buddy charged toward the truck, barking. Her son flew into her embrace while Buddy raced after the vehicle.

The driver swerved his pickup back toward the road, the rear tires spinning in the dirt and grass.

Even when the black truck bounced onto the pavement, Buddy continued to chase it.

Robbie twisted to watch the German shepherd. "Mom, I can't lose him."

"Cover your ears." Then Ella blew an ear-piercing whistle. "Buddy. Come."

The dog slowed and looked back at her.

"Come!" She shouted the command she'd heard Josiah use with his dog.

Buddy trotted toward her and Robbie. When the animal reached them, her son knelt and buried his face in the black fur on the German shepherd's neck.

Robbie peered up at Ella, tears running down his face. The sight of them confirmed that she would be staying with Josiah and his sister. She needed all the help she could get to keep her son safe.

"Let's go inside."

Her son rose, swiping the back of his hand across his cheeks. "Was that the man from the woods?"

"I couldn't tell. The truck's windows were tinted too dark, and there was no license plate."

"Is...is—" he gulped "—it my—" his chest rose and fell rapidly "—my dad?" The color drained from her son's face, and he continued to breathe fast.

Halfway back to the hangar, Ella stopped and squatted in front of Robbie and clasped his arms. "No. The photo you and the other boys identified looks nothing like your father."

"I'm scared."

So am I. "I won't let anything happen to you. I promise. Josiah has asked us to stay with him and his sister at their house. You remember his twin, Alex.

Her dog's name is Sadie. So you'll get to play with two dogs. That should be fun."

He nodded.

Ella fought to suppress her tears. If she broke down, it would upset Robbie. He hated seeing her cry. She'd done enough of that while living with her ex-husband. "I told David earlier that I was going to take at least a week off to spend time with you."

"Can we go camping?"

"Maybe."

"If we leave, the bad man can't get me."

She couldn't tell her son that wasn't always the case. If Keith ever found out where they were, he'd come after them, even though he'd lost his paternal rights because of his criminal activities working for a crime syndicate and his violence against her. "I'll talk with Josiah and the Detective Caldwell to see what's best."

The sound of a vehicle approaching drew Ella's attention. Josiah parked at the side of the hangar. When Robbie saw him climb from the Ford F-150, he snapped the leash on Buddy, then hurried toward Josiah. Ella watched her son run to him, pointing to the area where the black truck had driven off the road.

Even from a distance Ella could feel the anger pouring off the man. As he bridged the distance between them, a frown carved deep lines in his face. A storm greeted her in his blue eyes, but she didn't feel any of the fury was directed at her.

"Robbie, will you let David know I'm here with the supplies?" Josiah asked. "Take Buddy with you."

"Sure."

While her son led the German shepherd toward the hangar, Josiah asked, "Was it Foster?"

"I don't know. Maybe. The license plate was missing from the truck."

"Will you stay with Alex and me?"

"Yes."

"Can you leave now?"

"Right after I put the training session packets together. It shouldn't take me long."

"Good. I'll take you home so you can pack what you'll need. I'll have Robbie help David and me unload the truck while you finish up." He started for the hangar.

"Is this all right with Alex?"

"Are you kidding? She's thrilled to have others in that big old house she lives in."

"You don't live there?"

"I'm out back in the caretaker's cabin. Harry and Linda have a suite of rooms in the main house. They're more like family than employees." As David and Robbie emerged from the office door, Josiah caught her arm to pull her around to face him. "I'll call Thomas while you're packing. He'll want to know about this incident."

Ella nodded. She'd give whatever information she could to the police and pray it would help them find whoever was doing this to her and Robbie.

Later that evening, Josiah sat on the deck at the estate, watching Robbie play with both Buddy and Sadie. The sound of the boy's laughter penetrated the hard shell around Josiah's heart, put there to protect him from further pain after Lori's betrayal. He'd always wanted to be a father but had pushed that dream aside. Having a family meant trusting a woman enough to open up to her. He couldn't do that. If he couldn't give his heart to a woman, how in the world could they ever build a lasting relationship?

When Ella's son finally sank to the thick green grass and stretched out spread eagle, he called Sadie and Buddy to him. One dog lay on his right while the other sat on the left. Robbie stroked each one and stared up at the sky. It was good to see the child lose himself in the moment and forget for a while that someone was after him.

The French doors opened behind him, and he spied Ella coming toward him. Beautiful. Kind. But something was wrong. He could see it in her eyes, even before Robbie had been threatened. Had she been betrayed like him? She never talked about Robbie's father.

He turned his attention back to the boy playing between the dogs. He shouldn't care about Ella's past. But he did care. Why did she always look so sad?

"Well, we're all settled in our rooms." Ella sat in the lounge chair next to him.

"Good. I've decided to stay down the hall, and I want Buddy to sleep in Robbie's room, if that's all right with you."

"I couldn't say no. My son would disown me. He's so attached to Buddy. I need to get him his puppy soon or you'll have a problem when all this is over."

"We can go to the breeder on Tuesday. On Monday I'm driving to Fairbanks to talk with the team at Outdoor Alaska. I hope that you and Robbie will come with me. I'll only have to work a few hours, and then we can spend the rest of the time sightseeing or whatever else you'd like to do."

"Sounds wonderful. Robbie wants to go camping while I'm off. I'm not sure we should."

"If Robbie wants to camp out, we could do it here on the estate. We have woods." Josiah pointed toward the grove of trees along the back and side of his property. "It's not big, but it should give Robbie the sense of camping out in the forest."

"Is it safe?"

"It should be. We live in a gated community and even have private security guards patrolling the area. But the best security will be Buddy and Sadie. Nothing gets by them."

"Thanks. I don't want my son obsessed about the man stalking him. Did you notice on the drive here he didn't say a word?"

Josiah slid his hand over hers on the arm of her chair. "Yes. Young people generally never think anything bad will happen to them, and it is very sobering when that illusion is challenged or broken."

Ella rolled her head and shoulders. "And a challenge for parents to balance letting our children feel safe and really being safe. We want to protect them from every harm that comes their way, but we aren't with them 24/7. I know it was wrong for the boys to leave the camp area, but where were the counselors who were supposed to be keeping an eye on them?"

"It has to be doubly hard being a single parent. What happened to Robbie's father?"

She tensed, withdrawing her hand from his.

She began to rise when Josiah said, "I'm sorry. It's

none of my business. I just thought his father might be able to help."

A humorless laugh escaped her lips. "His father is no longer in his life. I'm telling you this so you don't ask about him anymore. It's a subject that distresses my son."

And Ella. Why? It was none of his business, and he usually respected a person's privacy, but he had a hard time letting it go.

"I'm sorry. I didn't mean to upset you."

She took a deep breath and tried to relax in the lounge chair, but her grasp on its arms indicated the tension still gripping her. "My philosophy is to look forward, not back. I can't change the past so I don't dwell there."

Easier said than done, he thought. He tried not to look backward, but what had happened to him was an intrinsic part of the man he was today. Ella's past was part of her present, too. She didn't have to tell him that Robbie's father was the one who'd hurt her so badly. He curled his hands into tight fists until they ached. Slowly he flexed them and practiced the relaxation techniques his counselor had taught him.

The sound of the French doors opening pulled Josiah's attention toward Thomas coming out on the deck. The fierce expression chiseled into his friend's face meant he was the bearer of bad news.

SIX

Ella saw Thomas heading for her. She straightened in her lounger on the deck at the Witherspoon estate. Not good news.

Thomas grabbed a chair and pulled it over to Ella and Josiah, checking to see where Robbie was.

Her son threw a Frisbee that Buddy caught in mid-air. "Did you all see that?" he yelled over to them.

"Yeah, both of the dogs love to catch Frisbees," Josiah answered while Thomas settled in his seat next to Ella. "So, Thomas, what happened?"

"A child a year older than Robbie, same hair coloring and height, has been taken by a man that fits Foster's description. A black truck like the one you described was identified near the abduction. We have an Amber Alert out on Seth London."

"Where did Foster get the black truck?" Ella asked, remembering that wasn't the description of the vehicle that his neighbor had reported stolen.

"It was reported stolen. He took the license off it, but we're looking at all black trucks, including those with plates, because we have a report of several license plates missing from a parking lot. We're also immediately investigating any car thefts in case he steals another one. Just like the first car, he probably won't keep the black truck long."

Josiah leaned forward, resting his elbows on his thighs. "What else?"

"We dug into Foster's past and found his record. He went crazy when his girlfriend sent her son to live with her grandparents, and he attacked her. The grandparents moved away from Alaska and disappeared. This month was the anniversary of when that happened."

"Was the child his?" Josiah glanced toward Ella.

Seeing the compassion in Josiah's gaze nearly undid her. Josiah was so different from the type of man Keith was, but then, she'd been fooled by her ex-husband, too.

Numb with all that had happened the past couple of days, Ella averted her head. She didn't want to hear about Foster, and yet she needed to know. The man had come after her son several times and might still try again.

"The girlfriend said no. Foster insisted he was the biological father and should have a say in where the boy lived. I'm joining the manhunt, but wanted you to hear what happened from me."

Finally Ella focused on the conversation. "It sounds as if he's gone crazy again."

"Yes. I'm speculating he saw the boys playing in the woods, and it made him snap. Michael, like Seth, looks similar to Robbie."

After the horror of my marriage, Lord, I don't know if I can do this. Ella lowered her head and twisted her hands in her lap.

"Do you need me to help with the hunt?"

The calm strength in Josiah's question reminded Ella that she wasn't alone this time. She had people who cared about her.

"We don't have an area narrowed down. Once Seth was taken into the truck, there was no scent for the dogs to follow. I'll let David know if we need Northern Frontier's resources. Right now the police are handling it, but David is on alert."

"I didn't receive a call from him. Did he say the training session tomorrow is still on?" Ella looked toward Josiah, his gaze ensnaring her. "Did he call you, Josiah?"

"No, not yet. I would have said something to you." Josiah's expression softened.

"He told me he's canceling it. He wants everyone ready if there's a need for civilians to search for Seth." Thomas stood.

"But he should have let me know," Ella said. "I usually make the calls when something is cancelled."

Thomas clasped Ella's shoulder and squeezed gently. "He knew I was on my way to talk with you. He wanted me to remind you that you're on vacation and he can handle everything for the next week."

Ella pursed her lips. "There are a lot of people to get in touch with."

"Bree is helping him. I want you to keep your son here. If Foster is fixating on kids like Robbie, he may still try to come after him. Michael and his mother have gone to Nome to visit some relatives." Thomas peered at Josiah. "I'll call with any news."

"I take it Alex knows about the most recent developments." Josiah got to his feet and walked to the railing of the deck.

"She wouldn't let me into the house until I told her."

"Yup, that's my sister. She wants to know what's going on before it happens."

When Thomas left, Ella stood beside Josiah at the railing. "I think if Buddy hadn't been with him, Robbie could have been Seth today."

"I hope someone sees Foster or the truck or something to give the police the break they need, but I am not going to let anything happen to Robbie."

Alex came out on the deck. "Dinner is ready. I would suggest you keep the TV and radio off. The story about Seth is all over the news. Tonight, while Buddy is staying with Robbie, I'm going to let Sadie loose downstairs to prowl. Ella, the alarm system here is top-notch. No one is going to get to Robbie with us around."

"Thanks. It's nice to have friends to turn to for help." Both Josiah and Alex had reassured her that she and Robbie weren't alone. She had to keep reminding herself of that. This wasn't the same as four years ago when she'd fled her husband. When she'd arrived in Alaska, she'd had no friends and a four-year-old to raise by herself.

Ella yelled out, "Robbie, it's time to come in."

Her son stopped before throwing the Frisbee and faced her, a dog on each side of him. "Do I hafta come in? We're having fun."

"Tuesday won't come fast enough. He needs a dog of his own," Ella murmured to Josiah and Alex, then shouted, "Yes. Now. Dinner is ready."

"It's still light out."

She shook her head. "It'll still be light at eleven o'clock when you'll be in bed."

Robbie shrugged his shoulders and plodded toward the steps to the deck with both dogs following closely. When he arrived in front of Ella, his mouth set in a pout, he said, "We were having so much fun."

"I know, and you'll be able to come out here tomorrow with Buddy and Sadie again, if you want."

"What about the training session? You told me we had to go there early."

"We're not going."

"Why not? You're in charge. David told me you were indi—indispensable."

Ella chewed on her lower lip. She shouldn't have said anything. Robbie didn't need to know about the little boy abducted today. He didn't need to worry. She'd do enough for the both of them. Then she remembered her granny telling her that when she began to worry, she should pray. Give it to God. Easier said than done. "I'm on vacation, remember? David wants me to start right away."

Robbie turned to Josiah. "Are you going?"

"Nope. I'm staying here, too."

A serious expression descended on Robbie's face, his forehead crinkling. "It's because of me and what happened yesterday."

Josiah nodded. "You're my priority and Buddy's."

"Yeah, he and Sadie are great. I can't wait to get my own dog."

"Soon." Ella started for the French doors. "I don't know about you two, but I'm starved. I didn't eat much at lunch."

Robbie peered up at Josiah and fell into step next to him. "That's because she ate while working at her desk."

"I've done that a few times and don't even remember what I ate an hour later. When we sit down for a meal, we should focus on the food and savor it." Josiah cocked a grin. "Or at least that's what my sister keeps telling me."

Robbie giggled. "I don't want a sister, but I'd love to have a brother."

Ella's cheeks flushed with heat. That wasn't going to happen, but at one time she'd wanted three or four children.

"My big sis isn't too bad, but I've always wanted a brother, too."

The laughter in Josiah's voice enticed her to glance toward him. His twinkling blue eyes fixed on her, and he winked.

Her face grew even warmer, and she hurried her pace to walk with Alex toward the dining room. She couldn't deny Josiah's good looks and kindness, but then Keith had been handsome and nice in the beginning. How could she ever let down her guard and trust any man?

Driving toward the Carter Kennels outside Fairbanks on Monday, Josiah took a peek at Robbie in the backseat, looking out the window. Ever since he'd told him he had something special planned for him, Robbie had kept his attention glued to the scenery as though that would tell him where he was going.

"When are we gonna be there? We've been driving

forever." Robbie turned forward. "I wonder if Buddy is doing okay."

"Robbie, you need to be patient." Ella shot her son a look that said *knock it off.* "That's the third time you've asked in the past forty minutes."

Josiah saw the mountain, at the base of which the kennel was located. "We're almost there."

"Where?"

"A surprise. After sitting around all morning at Outdoor Alaska, I thought we should do something I think you'll love."

"I miss Buddy."

"He needed a rest."

"He slept all night in my bed."

Josiah smiled and sliced a glance at Ella who rolled her eyes. "Yeah, but he was on guard duty."

"But he was snoring last night."

"Trust me, Robbie. You'll enjoy this."

When the large Carter Kennels sign came into view, Ella twisted toward her son. "This is a kennel for sled dogs. They train them here. One of the owners takes part in the Iditarod Race every year."

"Did he ever win?" The excitement in Robbie's voice infused the atmosphere in the truck.

Josiah chuckled. "He is a she, and Carrie has come in fifth and third. She told me next year she'll definitely win."

"I'd like to do something like that one day. I followed it this year."

"Yeah, your mom mentioned that to me when I asked her about coming here." Josiah pulled into the driveway. "Carrie has tours of the kennels in the summer, but she'll have time this afternoon to give us a private tour."

"She will? Yippee!" Robbie shot his arm into the air. "Will I be able to pet the dogs?"

"Carrie will have to let you know that. She's a trainer and has some great mushers." Josiah parked in front of a small black building where Carrie ran her business while the dogs stayed in a building off to the right.

As Carrie came outside, Josiah, Ella and Robbie climbed from the truck. Carrie was a fellow dog lover as well as a good customer of Outdoor Alaska. "It's nice to see you again." He shook the forty-year-old woman's hand.

"It's been a while since the Iditarod. You need to come out here more often. Great place to relax." Carrie turned her attention to Ella, then Robbie. A smile blossomed on her face as she greeted the boy. "You must be Robbie. I've been looking forward to meeting you today. Josiah said something about how much you love dogs and that you're a big fan of the Iditarod."

Eyes big, Robbie nodded his head. "Yes, ma'am. I was at the starting line this year rooting everyone on. One day I'd like to be at the finish line in Nome."

"Maybe you can drive a team one day."

Robbie grinned from ear to ear. "I hope so. I'm getting a puppy soon."

"An Alaskan husky?"

"No, a German shepherd from Buddy, Josiah's dog."

"Let's go meet my huskies." Carrie began walking toward the kennel area.

"I hope to train my dog to do search and rescue."

Robbie's voice drifted back to Josiah, who was trailing them with Ella next to him.

His chest swelled listening to the boy's words. He could remember when he was Robbie's age and thought anything was possible. He was going to conquer the world and save everyone. Then real life had intruded, and he grasped that he didn't need to do it on a grand scale but one person at a time. That realization had helped him deal with the past.

"I think I'm going to stand back and let my son enjoy the special time with Carrie. This is a dream come true for him."

"Good. Hopefully, after the past few days, this will take his mind off someone being after him."

Ella shook her head. "All because he reminds Foster of his ex-girlfriend's little boy. What is this world coming to?"

"Someone once told me that when I wake up in the morning, I should tell myself, 'This is the first day of the rest of my life.'" It was a piece of advice from the chaplain who'd visited him while he was recovering from his captivity.

"Has it helped?"

"When I remember to do it. Changing a mindset isn't always easy."

She looked off toward Robbie. "I know what you mean. I had someone suggest to me to start listing every day what I'm thankful for. To focus on what I have, not what I don't have."

"Has it helped?"

"When I remember to do it," she said with a laugh.

Robbie came running back to Ella. "Mom, I get to feed the dogs, then Carrie is going to show me how to hook up a sled. She is gonna let me go out on a sled run."

"How?"

"She says in the summer and fall she does A..." He scrunched his forehead and thought for a few seconds. "ATV training with her dogs when there isn't enough snow for a sled." Robbie rushed back to Carrie.

Ella released a long breath. "I have a feeling my son quoted her word for word."

"It's good to see him smiling so much."

Ella shifted toward Josiah. "All because of you. I can't tell you how much I appreciate your help. It hasn't been easy for me to accept help, but when your son's life is in jeopardy, you do what you have to do to keep him safe."

"You're a terrific mother."

She blushed.

"And Robbie knows it."

"There were moments this weekend when he wanted to do something I had to nix that I wasn't so sure."

"He shook off his disappointment and each time came up with something else to do." Josiah watched Robbie finish feeding the dogs, then walk toward a shed where he knew Carrie kept the dog sledding equipment. "I guess we'd better join them."

The faint red patches on her cheeks began to fade as she walked beside Josiah. "Thank you for showing Robbie some of Buddy's training. That took his mind off the fact that the activities at Northern Frontier were canceled on Saturday. When I told him last Friday he was going to attend with me, he was so excited. He didn't understand why it was called off, and I couldn't lie so I didn't tell him much of anything."

"It's hard trying to keep him protected from what's going on—Robbie's smart. I think he knows something is up."

"Yes, I'm afraid you're right. I want my dull life back."

As he strolled across the compound, he took her hand and peered down at her. "Dull is good." He'd learned excitement wasn't all it was cracked up to be. He'd joined an elite team in the Marines because he'd wanted more action. Once, when he'd been injured and had desk duty for a month, he'd become so restless he'd tried to get the doctor to clear him for active duty early.

When he and Ella were a couple of yards away, Robbie held up a harness. "I get to put this on a dog, then help set up the tug line and gang line."

"Great," she said to her son, then leaned closer to Josiah. "I know what he's going to be doing the rest of the summer. Reading everything he can find on sled dogs."

"Don't be surprised if he becomes the youngest competitor in the race."

For a few seconds Ella blinked as though surprised. All traces of enthusiasm left her expression as she swallowed hard.

"Is something wrong?"

She angled away from him. "No, nothing's wrong, so long as my son is safe."

Strange. Something didn't fit. He started to ask her about what she'd said, but quickly decided it wasn't his concern. Obviously she didn't want to share it with him, and that bothered him.

Ella opened the garage door to the kitchen, so Josiah could carry Robbie, who was sound asleep, into the house. Buddy and Sadie greeted them at the door when they entered.

Positioned at the sink, Linda glanced at them.

"Where's Alex?" Josiah asked as he crossed the room.

"In the den. She came home right before dinner. I can fix you some leftovers if you want."

"Thanks. We ate in Fairbanks not that long ago." Josiah headed for the hallway.

Ella followed him. "Will you carry him upstairs and put him on his bed? I doubt he'll wake up before morning. He's worn out from today." Josiah had gone out of his way to make the outing to Fairbanks special for Robbie. That was another reason she was attracted to Josiah when she shouldn't be. He cared about her son, and Robbie hung on to every word Josiah said. Robbie's father had never spent any time with his son.

After he placed Robbie in his room, he backed away. "I'm going to let Alex know how my visit to the store went today."

"I'll be down in a little bit. I'm tired but not ready for bed." Ella removed Robbie's tennis shoes while Buddy settled on the floor next to the bed.

She put a light sheet over her son, then smoothed some of his hair from his face. When she did that when he was awake, he'd act as though he was too old to have his mother fuss over him. In a couple of months he would be nine.

What if I have to leave Alaska?

Ella crossed to the window to pull the shades half-way down but stopped and looked out onto the back-yard toward the stand of birch and spruce trees at the rear of the property. It was eleven o'clock at night, and the sun was finally setting but would rise before five. At least she didn't have to worry about a man peeking in at her son sleeping here. Chills shivered up her spine as she thought back to Thursday night, when Foster had done just that. She tugged the blinds another several inches down.

She dug her cell phone out of her jeans pocket and checked to see if David or Thomas had left her a message. Nothing. Still no sign of Foster. People headed into the wilderness all the time to disappear from civilization. What would she do if the police never found Foster?

She'd left Georgia because of Keith. She didn't want to leave Alaska because of Foster.

Her son mumbled something she couldn't understand and rolled over on the bed.

"Robbie," she whispered, checking to see if he was awake.

When she saw his eyes were closed, she released her pent-up breath and headed into the hallway. Her stomach rumbled. She'd worked up an appetite after walking along Chena River at the Fairbanks Downtown Market after visiting the Carter Kennels. She'd enjoyed the music, sampling some of the food and the atmosphere. For a while, she'd felt free, as though they hadn't a care in the world, and she and Robbie were spending the day with a wonderful man under normal circumstances.

Now she wasn't even sure if that would ever be possible. After Keith had been put into the Witness Security Program because he'd turned state's evidence against the crime syndicate he'd worked for, she had no idea where he was. She didn't know if he was in a prison or out there somewhere with a new identity.

Robbie and I are totally in Your hands, Lord. She repeated the prayer as she descended the stairs to the first floor. She'd done everything she could to vanish. She followed the New Life Organization's instructions—as though she and Robbie were in WitSec like Keith—and so far it had worked for four years.

As she neared the den, she heard Josiah ask, "What did David have to say?"

"He's calling everyone about meeting to help with the search now that the state police have found the black truck. What are you going to do?"

Ella paused before entering to hear what Josiah would say to Alex without her around. She didn't want to keep him from doing what he should do. Josiah and Buddy were a great SAR team.

"I'm staying here. My first priority is Ella and Robbie."

"I'm going. You know how I feel about any child that's missing."

"You should. I would go, too, but—"

"Good, because I'm going to be involved," Ella said from the den's entrance.

Josiah looked at Ella. "You can't. What about your son?"

"Robbie will also go. He'll help me at the command center. David will be there, so we'll be fine, but they're going to need all the trained dogs with good handlers if they're going to locate Seth." When Josiah frowned and started to say something, she set her hand on her waist. "And honestly, do you see Foster walking into the command center to take Robbie? We know what the man looks like. With the police crawling around the area, he won't."

Josiah exchanged a glance with Alex. "Okay, but only if David agrees."

She put her other hand on her waist and narrowed her eyes on Josiah. "You're hoping he says no, aren't you?"

He grinned. "Of course. That's why bosses get paid big bucks."

"He volunteers his services just like you."

"But he has the fancy title."

Alex laughed and rose from the couch. "I'm going to let Sadie outside to check the grounds, then I'm off to bed. Four o'clock will be here soon enough."

Ella sat where Alex had been. "So tell me, what have the police found?"

"The black truck used to kidnap Seth was found off Eagle River Road half an hour ago. The area around there is wooded and vast. Although it's going to be dark soon, the K-9 unit is searching the immediate area, but as soon as it's light, they want us in place so we can blanket the vicinity."

"Maybe they'll find Foster and Seth beforehand." Ella shifted to face Josiah at the other end of the couch.

"I hope so, but there are a lot of places to hide, and the Eagle River is nearby. He could try using the water to throw the dogs off."

"Even in July the water is ice-cold."

"There's a chance Foster isn't even there or Seth. But it has to be searched."

"And you need to be there. Robbie and I are going, too. This is why I work for Northern Frontier Search and Rescue. I'm good at running the command center and keeping track of where our volunteers are." She scooted closer to Josiah until they were inches apart. "I'm going, and David can't do anything about it once I'm there."

His blue eyes softened. "Fine. Both Alex and I are dedicated to searching for any child missing, no matter when or where."

Ella wanted to melt under his perusal. "I know. I've seen your dedication."

"Once when we were eleven, a friend went missing. The conditions weren't the best. Only about half the searchers needed arrived. By the time he was found, he'd died. I'll never forget that. That's why I got serious about survival in the wilderness and trained Buddy to be a SAR dog."

"I'm so sorry about your friend."

"The worst part was I couldn't do anything to help him."

The more she got to know Josiah, the more she realized how much integrity he had. But she still felt that he kept a part of himself bottled up and hidden from the world.

She laid her hand over his on the couch. "You were only a kid. Robbie keeps wondering why he can't help search."

His gaze locked with hers, and she felt like she was drowning in those blue depths. "I understand why kids don't join search teams. In Alaska, tragedy can happen quickly. But even knowing the reason doesn't mean it didn't affect me."

The urge to cup the rugged line of his jaw inundated her. She grappled for a subject that would keep her from speculating how it would feel to kiss him. "I wonder how capable Foster is in the backcountry." She relaxed against the cushion, slipping her hand from his. Too dangerous.

"Let's hope he makes a mistake and gets caught."

"That's what I'll be praying for while you all are out searching."

He rose, holding his arm out toward her. "We'd better get some rest. We'll have to leave in less than four hours."

When he pulled her to her feet, she came up close against him. He grasped her, their gazes bound as though ropes held them together. He brushed his fingers through her hair, then cupped her face. He bent toward her, then his mouth claimed hers in a kiss. Suddenly, her legs felt like jelly, so she gripped his arms to keep herself upright.

A series of barks broke them apart as Ella looked toward the door.

"That's Buddy," Josiah said, as he charged from the room.

SEVEN

Could someone have gotten into the house?

Josiah raced for the stairs, taking them two at a time with Ella right behind him. He hit the second-floor landing at a dead run. When he reached Robbie's room and started to open the door, the barking ceased. He slammed into the room, his heart galloping as fast as a polar bear after its prey. Nearly colliding with Robbie a few feet inside, Josiah skidded to a halt.

The boy stood in the center of the room, his arms straight at his sides, a blank expression on his face as he stared into space. Buddy nudged his hand. Nothing. Josiah glanced toward the hallway, not sure what to do.

Ella hurried inside, took one look at her son and relaxed the tensed set of her body. "Occasionally in the past, he has sleepwalked. He used to do it more when he was younger. The doctor thought he'd outgrow it as he got older." She kneaded her neck. "It's been six months since he did it, so I thought he finally had. Usually the age range for sleepwalking in children is between four and eight years old, and he'll be nine in September."

of David's briefing. Ella started back toward the tent pitched near the nature center. Her gaze immediately zeroed in on her son, who hadn't left Josiah's side. In the past days, Robbie had followed Josiah around everywhere. They'd bonded almost overnight, and that scared her. What would happen when Foster was found and they went back to their life without Josiah and Buddy? The thought added a chill to the cool morning air. She zipped up her light parka as though that would warm her. She had a feeling that when Josiah went on with his life, he'd leave a hole in both her life and Robbie's.

Memories of their kiss the night before haunted her again. She'd barely slept because he'd filled her thoughts. She would not fall in love with Josiah. She'd fallen in love with Keith, and her life had become a nightmare not long after the wedding. How could she tell Josiah about her ex-husband?

The searchers began grouping with their team leaders. Josiah knelt in front of Robbie and clasped her son's arm. He said something too quietly for her to hear, but whatever Josiah told Robbie, it turned his frown into a grin.

Robbie hugged Josiah, then gave him Buddy's leash. Josiah rose, and they exchanged high fives. Emotions overflowed her throat. She swallowed hard as Josiah looked around, then caught sight of her. He smiled and waved. Her son had missed out on a male role model. Even when Keith had been around, he hadn't really been a part of Robbie's life. How would she ever be able to make it up to her son for her bad judgment concerning her ex-husband?

"I've noticed you're one of the organizers. Could

"Then I'm glad Buddy was here. If Robbie had left his room, he could have fallen down the stairs."

"He wanders around his bedroom, and I'd often find him asleep on the floor the next morning." Ella guided Robbie back to the bed and tucked him in. "He doesn't realize he's done it, even when he wakes up in a different place."

Josiah stood with Ella by the door to make sure Robbie didn't get up. She curled her hand around his and took deep breaths.

"I think he's fine."

"If not, Buddy will let us know."

In the hallway she faced Josiah. "You and your sister have done so much for Robbie and me. I can't thank you enough."

"You don't have to thank me. I do it because it's the right thing to do. You can trust me. I won't do anything to hurt you or Robbie."

"I know."

He studied her for a moment. "Do you really? I'm not sure you do."

"Why do you say that? I wouldn't be here if I didn't."

"Someone has hurt you, made you wary. I certainly understand that. I just wanted you to know where I stand."

She pursed her lips and stared at his shirtfront. "I won't deny that I've been hurt. I divorced a man who didn't love or care about his son." She took several steps to her bedroom door. "Good night. I'll see you in a few hours."

Josiah watched her disappear inside the room, closing the door quietly while her body language screamed tension. It was obvious the man didn't love or care about Ella, either. Under different circumstances, he would pursue Ella, but he didn't have any business getting involved with a woman. The last one had left her mark on his heart.

By five in the morning the next day, Ella had signed in most of the searchers at Northern Frontier Search and Rescue. She counted only three left in line.

"Mom, why can't I go out with Josiah? I want to learn all I can about having a SAR dog." Robbie whined as he sat next to her at the check-in table for Seth's searchers.

"Because you'll remain glued to my side the whole time." She took the check-in form from another searcher and gave instructions to the next person.

"But I want to help!"

"You are helping. I wouldn't be here if you weren't with me. You'll be able to search when you're older."

Robbie pouted. "I'm always too young. When I get my puppy, I'm gonna start working with him right away. At least I can do that." He slumped against the canvas back of the chair.

"That's a good plan." Ella took the check-in form from the last searcher. It was two minutes until David would brief the search teams on the situation and objectives.

Ella rose and stretched.

Robbie jumped to his feet. "Can I hang out with Josiah until he leaves?"

She nodded, realizing a good part of the day would be boring for her son. Maybe she shouldn't have come, but that would have meant one less team of handlers

and dogs. Like Josiah said last night, this was the right thing to do.

She watched her son hurry to the tent and find Josiah standing next to Buddy. A couple of seconds later, he handed her son his dog's leash, and Robbie grinned from ear to ear.

With a deep sigh, she made her way to the tent, wanting to listen to the briefing but still keep an eye on the check-in table. Two searchers had yet to show up—a husband-and-wife team. She hoped nothing had happened to them. They could use everyone to help the state troopers overseeing the search for Seth.

David signaled for quiet. "I've just been updated. We'll be searching this area." He pointed to area south and west of Eagle River Nature Center, where their staging area was. "A trail from the truck Foster used in the abduction of Seth London headed away from the center toward the south. From the tracks the police have found, there's evidence that Foster went into the backcountry with Seth but the boy didn't come out. A vehicle was reported stolen half an hour ago. They believe, based on the footprints, that Foster took the car. There was no evidence the child was with him. Our job is to search that area and pray we find the child alive."

As David continued to fill the searchers in on what they would do, Ella spotted the couple arriving and walked back to the table to check them in.

"We're sorry. We had a flat tire."

"I'm so glad you are here and safe. David is just finishing up with the group now. Talk to him, and he'll give you the spiel and instructions."

They nodded, then rushed to catch the last part

you answer a few questions?" a woman asked from behind Ella.

When Ella pivoted toward her, she realized a cameraman was standing behind the woman, as well as a photographer snapping pictures as the searchers prepared to leave.

"We just arrived and didn't catch the briefing." The young lady she recognized from a local television station held a microphone up for Ella to reply.

She froze. She always worked way behind the scenes of a search, and usually kept track of any media covering the rescue. Being fixated on Josiah's relationship with her son had caused her to let down her guard.

Ella pointed toward the tent. "You'll want to talk with David Stone. He can answer your questions."

"Thank you." The woman and her cameraman headed for the tent.

But the photographer stayed behind and continued taking pictures. This rescue would generate a lot more media coverage than usual because of the nature of the story. She quickly put some of the searchers between her and the reporters, grabbed Robbie, then headed around the nature center.

She wasn't worried about the TV reporter, because the station wouldn't air anything that didn't contribute to the story, but she would have to stay away from the photographers. For all she knew, her husband could be dead. He'd certainly angered a lot of people, but she wasn't going to take a chance.

Hours ago after being airlifted to one of the sites where a set of tracks, which the authorities thought were Foster's and Seth's, had been discovered, Josiah gave Buddy a long leash. Josiah kept his gaze trained on his surroundings for any footprints to compare with what he'd seen at the start. He prayed to the Lord to guide his steps and help him find the child. He knew of the dangers in the wilderness—bears, moose, freezing water, falling on the rough trail.

The other searchers were behind the handlers with their dogs, covering the ground much more slowly, looking for any signs to help them. To Josiah's left, his sister and Sadie were following Eagle River. He hoped the child hadn't fallen into the ice-cold river or the many creeks feeding into it. From what he'd heard in the briefing, Seth didn't swim well.

Buddy reached one creek crossing that branched out over a large area. Josiah and his dog navigated to the other side by using downed logs and stepping-stones.

Buddy was following Seth's scent from an article of clothing while Sadie was following Foster's. So far the two dogs were going the same direction.

Using an SAR satellite phone, Josiah called in to headquarters. "We've come about three miles from the drop-off site. It looks like Foster and Seth crossed a creek here. We'll pick up their scent on the other side."

"The other teams are calling in, too. So far nothing." Ella's voice sounded strained.

"Is everything all right?"

"Yes, just a media circus here. Thankfully David is the spokesperson."

"I'll check in later."

"Be careful. No sightings of Foster or the car he

stole at the parking lot in Girdwood, but the police have confirmed from video feeds that Foster took the vehicle. No sign of Seth in the tapes."

He gritted his teeth, hoping the boy was still alive. "How's Robbie?"

"Asleep right now in the tent. Take care and don't worry. David and Bree are keeping a good eye on us."

"Okay. Bye." As he put his phone into his backpack, visions of them kissing last night appeared in his mind. He was starting to care about her more and more with each day they spent together.

Josiah stepped up to the water. The morning had barely started to warm up. "I'll go first," he said to Alex. "Make sure we can get across."

As he hopped from one rock to another, he slipped and his leg went down into the icy water. He sucked in a deep breath and yanked his foot free. Buddy sat on the other side of the stream, waiting only yards away.

When he reached the other side, Josiah waved to Alex. His sister crossed the creek, learning from his misstep to go another route. As she and Sadie joined him, he said to Buddy, "Search." There weren't too many ways to cross the creek, so he hoped they'd pick up the scent quickly.

His German shepherd sniffed the ground until Josiah finally said, "Looks like Buddy hasn't picked up the scent yet. I'm heading this way."

"I'll go the opposite direction," Alex said.

Josiah only went five yards before Buddy picked up the trail. He gave a loud whistle to indicate that Alex should join him. When she did, Sadie also found Foster's scent.

"What made Foster deviate from the trail?" Josiah looked around at the dense underbrush and forest surrounding the area. "Maybe there was someone he wanted to avoid."

"Whatever the reason, this is the way we go. They're still together."

"This doesn't make sense. Why is Foster even bringing Seth here? This isn't isolated."

"This is pure speculation," Alex said, "but he used to think of his girlfriend's son as his own. What if he's trying to do stuff he would have done with a son?"

For the next hour, he and Alex went along the trail part of the way then off it then back on the path. When the vegetation thickened, Josiah suddenly veered away from Alex.

"Seth is going this way." He glanced back at his sister.

She took several more steps before Sadie dived into the thicket, as though Foster was chasing after Seth. Off the trail Alex and Josiah came together about forty yards into the thick woods, following the course of a creek upstream.

Josiah let Buddy off the leash so he could go faster through the brush. A couple of minutes later, his German shepherd barked, followed by Sadie. Although Foster had been sighted in Girdwood, Josiah removed his gun. As a soldier he'd learned it was better to be prepared rather than surprised.

He forged through the vegetation, spotting a small green tent nestled among the trees. Alex and he exchanged looks. He motioned for her to stay in case Foster had somehow returned. Taking off his backpack, Josiah left it next to Alex and crept forward, always keeping his eyes open for a bear.

When he reached the tent, he didn't go in through the front but uprooted one of the stakes on the side and lifted the tarp. Inside, Josiah saw Seth, who was terrified. The boy's mouth had duct tape over it, and his feet and hands were bound, but he was alive.

"I'm here to rescue you, Seth. Your parents have been worried sick." Buddy barked again and Josiah added, "That's my dog. He found you. I'm going to come in through the opening and untie you. Okay?"

The child's eyes were still round as saucers, but he nodded and struggled to sit up.

Josiah called out to Alex, "I found Seth alive. Call base and let them know."

Later that evening, Ella entered the den, tired but so glad that Seth was back with his parents, dehydrated but unharmed. "Where's Alex?"

"She went to bed. She has to get up early for a meeting at the store." With feet propped up on the coffee table in front of the navy blue leather couch, he nursed a tall glass of iced tea while watching TV. He turned the sound down and patted the cushion next to him. "Sit. Relax. It's been a long day."

"Alex is okay that you aren't going into work tomorrow?" She sat at the opposite end of the sofa from Josiah. Getting any closer was just too dangerous. She still couldn't get their kiss out of her thoughts.

Josiah chuckled. "She's fine. Besides, I have a long list of suppliers I'll be contacting tomorrow. I often work from here. That's the beauty of my job. I don't always have to go into the office."

"I was hoping the police would have found Foster by now."

"He'll be found. His photo has been plastered all over town, as well as the description of the car he's driving. Roadblocks have been set up, and all ways to leave the area are under surveillance. He took a child. A lot of people are eager to bring him in. You and Robbie will be home in no time."

Home. The house she lived in now was the first place she'd called that since she'd left her childhood home and married Keith. Sometimes she prayed that she could go back to Georgia and see her parents, but that wouldn't be smart. "I hope so. I hate being an imposition on you and Alex."

"I've told you a thousand times. You aren't."

She relaxed against the couch and sighed. "I'm bone tired, but I wouldn't have traded seeing Seth reunited with his parents for anything. The other day I had a taste of what it feels like to have your child missing. A parent's worst nightmare."

"If it wasn't for Buddy and Sadie, I'm not sure he would have been found before his dehydration became serious. The Lord was with us today."

"Foster must be crazy. I can't believe he brought Seth all the way out there and then left him. What if a bear had come upon the child?"

"Thankfully one didn't. Thomas thinks that Foster is falling apart, which will probably cause him to make a mistake. After Thomas talked with Seth, he told me that Foster had wanted to share a camping trip with the child. Foster had kept saying how he'd promised him one, and finally they could go. I think Alex had it right that Foster thought of Seth as the son who was taken away from him."

"What if he goes after another child?"

"That's definitely a possibility. That's why the news is making it clear to parents to watch their children, especially young boys." Josiah angled himself on the couch toward Ella. "When Thomas went through Foster's apartment, they found a closet with walls plastered with pictures of his ex-girlfriend's son."

"When did this happen?"

"Right after they identified him, they went through it from top to bottom, trying to find a lead."

She straightened. "That was days ago. Why didn't you tell me this sooner?"

A tic in his jaw jerked. His hand on the couch fisted.

"What are you not telling me?"

Silence.

"I'm not leaving until you tell me. What are you hiding from me?"

"In my defense, I didn't hear this from Thomas until late Sunday night after you had gone to sleep. Thomas called to give me an update on the investigation and told me then about the closet..." He uncurled his hand then balled it again. "He had taken a few photos of Robbie, and they were posted over the other boy."

Ella heard his words, but it took a moment for their meaning to register in her mind. She bolted to her feet and rotated toward him. "You should have woken me up and told me this right away!"

"Sunday was the first time you'd gotten a good night's rest. You had been functioning on minimal sleep for days."

"Then yesterday."

"There was never a right moment. I wasn't going to dampen our outing to Fairbanks, then the truck Foster had stolen was found."

"I can think of a few." Ella began to pace. "How many pictures? Where were they taken?"

"There were four. Taken at the day camp, and his friends were in them, so they could have been shot because of one of them. Remember Michael is similar to Robbie and Seth in size and coloring."

She stopped and faced him, her arms ramrod straight at her sides. "And yet, Foster came to my house and peeped into Robbie's bedroom. I would say that meant he'd singled out Robbie."

"With all that's been going on with Seth, I didn't want to add to your worry."

"I'm a grown woman who's been on her own for years. I can take care of myself." Had she been lured into a false sense of safety when she of all people should realize no one was ever totally safe? She got up and started pacing, wound too tight to sit and relax.

"You don't always have to do everything by yourself." He rose and blocked her path. "I've learned the hard way there are some things I can't control. In fact, a good part of life is out of my control. But I can control how I react, what I think."

She began to go around Josiah, but suddenly the fight drained out of her. "I know, and I'm working on it, but with all that's happened lately, past fears have a hold on me."

He clasped her hand, threading his fingers through hers. "What fears?"

For a moment she contemplated telling him about Keith, but the words clogged her throat and she couldn't. "One I need to put to rest," she finally murmured, lowering her gaze.

He lifted her chin until she looked in his eyes. "We all have fears we need to put to rest. Easy to say. Hard to do."

What are yours? she wondered. She exhaled and stepped back, her hand slipping from his. "I'm trying not to worry all the time. To give those concerns to the Lord and trust more, but it's a constant battle."

"Faith can be." Josiah took his seat on the couch.

Ella remained standing in front of the fireplace. "Please let me know if you hear something else from Thomas right away. I'm not as fragile as you think I am."

"On the contrary, I think you're a strong woman. You help others. You're raising a wonderful son by yourself. There are many qualities about you that I admire."

The heat of a blush slowly swept over her face. If he only knew about her past. It had taken her years to get away from Keith. She'd kept thinking things would change, and when she realized they wouldn't, she'd discovered how controlling her ex-husband really was.

Needing to turn the conversation away from her, she searched for a topic. When she spied Josiah yawning, she said, "I can't believe you aren't asleep after the day you've had, hiking for miles, carrying Seth to the helicopter pickup site. Why are you still up?"

"I wanted to watch the news. See if anything has happened."

"Doesn't Thomas keep you updated?"

"When he has the time. I didn't know about the pictures right away."

She sat at the other end of the couch. "Probably not a bad idea. I don't know what I'll do if Foster isn't found soon. I can't keep taking time off, and I need my job."

"We'll deal with that when the time comes."

We'll? Like a couple? The idea struck panic in her but also gave her a sense of comfort. For the first time in years she actually didn't feel alone. She'd purposefully held part of herself back from others, and the thought Josiah could break down all her barriers frightened her.

He leaned forward, picked up the remote and turned up the sound. "I figure they'll lead with Seth's story."

But the anchorman cut to a national story first. Ella slid a gaze toward him and found him watching her.

A smile lifted the corners of his mouth. "Maybe we'll see our pictures on the news. Our fifteen seconds of fame."

"Maybe you. I seem to remember a reporter sticking a microphone in your face when you hopped down from that helicopter."

"Earlier today, there was a happy ending to the kidnapping of Seth London. He's been returned home safely to his parents," the anchorman said, the picture on the television switching from him to one of Seth's parents hugging their child.

Then Mr. London made a statement to the press praising the searchers who found Seth.

A video of Josiah as he climbed down from the

helicopter came on, followed by him saying, "My dog is the one who found Seth. I was just tagging along."

Ella smiled. "You're about as comfortable as I am in the limelight."

"I'd rather face a grizzly than a reporter."

She laughed, her earlier tension melting away while David came on the screen and told the reporter about his dedicated search and rescue team members. Then a picture of her with Robbie flashed on the TV with a voice saying, "This is one particularly hard-working member, Ella Jackson, with her son, Robbie."

She heard Josiah chuckling. "And there's your fifteen seconds of fame." But it sounded as if he was talking from the end of a long tunnel, his voice echoing off the concrete walls.

Her face—and Robbie's—was on the evening news. For everyone to see. What if the national news picked up the story? And Keith saw it?

EIGHT

Ella's face turned as pale as her white shirt, and her eyes grew as large as saucers.

Josiah moved closer to her on the couch. "Ella? Are you okay?" He didn't understand what was wrong. He laid his hand on her arm and said, "I know you'd rather work behind the scenes, but you are just as important as the people out searching. I'm so glad you got some recognition for your contribution."

She yanked her arm from his grasp. "I didn't know they took that photo of me and Robbie. They shouldn't have."

The frantic ring to her words worried him. Something else was going on here. "Ella, what's really wrong? This is good publicity for Northern Frontier Search and Rescue. I won't be surprised if donations flood the office after this piece."

Her hands began to tremble, and she hugged herself, tucking her fingers under her arms. "This is *not* good." She shot to her feet. "I've got to leave Anchorage. I can't stay. It's not safe."

She ran for the hallway. Josiah hurried after her and caught up with her in the foyer.

He held both her hands in his, and waited until she

made eye contact to say, "Foster is *not* going to get to Robbie. You're safe."

"No. You don't understand."

"Make me understand." He wanted to hold her until she calmed down, but she strained away from him.

"I need to go home and pack. Leave. Right now."

"Why, Ella? What are you afraid of? I promise I will never let Foster hurt your son or you."

She shook her head. "It's not just Foster I'm afraid of." Her eyes widened even more. She snapped her mouth closed, swept around and raced up the staircase.

Josiah went after her, taking the steps two at a time. Inside her bedroom, she swung her suitcase up on the bed and hurried toward the closet. He stood in the doorway, watching her, not sure what he should do.

She was worried the piece about Seth's rescue would be on national TV. Why? Her ex-husband? From the one comment she'd made about him, he hadn't been a good father to Robbie. Was there more?

Suddenly Ella came to a halt between the closet and bed, a blouse and sweater in her hand. Her gaze fell on him as the clothes floated to the floor. Tears glistened in her eyes, full of fear.

Whatever it was, she was terrified.

He covered the distance to her and embraced her, tugging her against him as though he could somehow erase the panic by holding her. He would do anything to take away that sense of alarm, but at the moment he felt helpless as he listened to her cry against his shoulder.

He stroked her back, her sobs breaking down the

wall he hid behind. He closed his eyes and sent a prayer for help to the Lord.

When her tears stopped, he loosened his hold enough to lean away to look at her. "Ella." He waited until she focused on him. "Tell me what is wrong. If I can help, I will. Please."

Ella blinked and moved back, swiping at her cheeks. "I'm sorry for that."

"Don't be. We all hit a wall at different times in our life." He, more than most, had realized that the hard way.

"That's exactly how I feel. For years I've held my emotions inside, and suddenly they just needed to be released."

He drew her to a love seat nearby, sat and pulled her down next to him. "Maybe it's time you share all these emotions with someone. I get the feeling you haven't."

"Not for four years." She wanted to tell him her story, but she was afraid. And yet, the words *tell him* bounced around her mind. Could she trust him? She was so tired of going it alone.

"You don't have to say anything, but whatever you tell me I'll keep in confidence. I know what it feels like to need to talk, but something holds you back."

She started to ask him about it but realized this wasn't the time. Taking a cleansing breath, she stared at her laced fingers in her lap and murmured, "My ex-husband can't find me. If he does, he'll kill me." Slowly, unsure of his reaction, she peered into his eyes—full of compassion and something else. Anger?

A nerve twitched in his jaw as he covered her clasped hands with his. "Why do you think that?"

"I'm the one who turned him in to the police for his illegal activities. Once he was in jail, I ran from him, taking Robbie with me. Through the New Life Organization, a group that helps abused women leave their husbands, I was able to divorce him and get complete custody of my son. If it hadn't been for them, I don't know what I would have done."

Although Josiah's expression was fierce, his touch against her hands was gentle. "Did he ever hit you or Robbie?"

"Only me, but he'd come close to hitting Robbie toward the end. I'd tried to leave him a couple of times, and he always found me, dragged me back home. I discovered the first time I ran away that his associates were ruthless and would stop at nothing to get what they wanted. That was how Keith was, too."

"Then how were you able to finally get away from him?"

"I arranged through our maid to give the police information I'd discovered about Keith's criminal activities. She was a lifesaver and the reason I'm a Christian. I don't know what I would have done without Rosa. Everyone else who worked for my husband was terrified of him. God sent her to me when I needed her."

"What happened to her?"

Ella could remember so vividly when she'd said goodbye to Rosa. The emotions of that parting inundated her, and the tears welled up in her throat. "I gave her some money, and she went back to her own country. Originally she was going to come with me, but she was homesick. I miss her so much, but for

Robbie's sake, I've cut off all ties to my past, including my parents."

"If you turned your ex-husband into the police, why isn't he in prison? Or was he released?"

"He was charged but never went to trial. I found out that he had turned the state's evidence against the crime organization he was part of."

"Is he in the witness security program now?"

"No one will tell me for sure, but I know he disappeared. I imagine he is, but he has his own problems. The people he worked for won't hesitate to kill him if they find him. I've scoured the internet for any trace of him and never found anything."

"And now you're afraid he might see that photo of you and know where you are?"

She nodded. "I've always been so careful not to have my picture taken. Nowadays one photo can live on the internet forever. TV networks and newspapers all put their photos and videos up on the internet. Now I don't know what to do."

"You think he's still looking for you?"

"I have to think he is. To ignore that possibility could mean tragedy. When Robbie went missing, my first thought was that Keith had found us and he'd kidnapped him. For a few seconds, I was relieved it was Foster. But he's become a problem in his own right." The thumping of her heart made breathing difficult.

"Foster will be found."

"I'm not so sure. He's been eluding the police for a while now. Don't forget, Alaska is a big state."

Josiah frowned. "True, but it seems as though he's losing all sense of reality. He'll make a mistake soon and get caught. I have to believe that."

"Because the alternative is that there might be two people who want to come after Robbie?"

"We have some dedicated people looking for Foster, and now the public is involved."

"I hope we catch him. I love living here, and I don't want to run again. I'm tired of running."

He pulled her toward him, and slipped his arm around her. She nestled against him. "Your ex-husband has his own problems. If he has powerful people coming after him, then I can't see him coming after you. He'll do what he needs to do to protect himself. Drawing attention to himself could alert the criminals he turned against."

"Keith always put himself first, so you're probably right." She laid her head against his shoulder and savored the moment. Right now this was the safest place for her and Robbie. She needed to practice putting herself in the Lord's hands, because the alternative was living a life of fear.

"You'll see. After Foster is captured, everything will return to normal." His hand rubbed up and down her back.

Normal? She wasn't sure she knew what that was. Her life hadn't been normal for years.

"But one thing I promise you. Your past is safe with me. You don't have to do this alone."

She'd always dreamed of someone saying that to her, but Josiah had his own problems that he kept secret. Even though she'd become a very private person out of necessity, she'd never fall in love with someone hiding part of himself. Not after Keith. She couldn't go through that again.

"I think we need to plan something fun to do after Foster is caught. Any suggestions?"

"I think Robbie would like a camping trip."

"What about you?"

"Whatever Robbie wants, I want. But I have to warn you. I'm a complete novice. I'm not even sure I can put up a tent."

"We can remedy that. I'll make my business calls tomorrow, and then we'll set a tent up in the backyard. You need to know how and so does Robbie, especially if we do go camping."

"That would be great."

"Okay, now, what would you like to do for yourself?"

"Robbie being happy is something for myself."

"What's your heart's desire?"

The fact that Josiah had even bothered to ask her that stunned her. Not once had Keith or anyone else asked her. She couldn't tell him her heart's desire was to be loved unconditionally. "I'd love to go out to dinner at Celeste's. I'd never be able to afford it, though," she said instead.

"Celeste's. Done. I suspect that isn't really what your heart's desire is, but I can understand your reluctance to reveal the truth." He smiled, a gleam in his eyes that made her feel cherished. "I hope one day you'll be able to tell me. It's hard being alone."

The way he said that last sentence held a wealth of loneliness. She wanted to ask him what had happened, but she swallowed the question and pushed to her feet. "Thank you for your help."

A glint of sadness winked at her as he rose, clasped

her upper arms and leaned toward her to kiss her forehead. "Good night."

Too good to be true. Remember how Keith had been such a gentleman until you got married? Like Dr. Jekyll and Mr. Hyde.

She squeezed her eyes shut, the click of the door closing indicating he was gone from the room. But not from her thoughts—or her heart.

Josiah watched Robbie help Ella put up the tent in his backyard. The sight of them working together was beautiful to see. After hearing about Ella's ex-husband, he admired her even more. But he worried that he had too much baggage to be the right man for her. She needed someone who didn't have occasional panic attacks, who didn't wake up soaked in sweat in the middle of the night from a nightmare, who was afraid to ever give his heart to another.

"Mom, you also forgot to tie the poles together at the top. If you don't, it might collapse on you."

After following her son's instruction, Ella moved back from the tent. "Is this what you mean?"

"Yup. Good job." Robbie crawled inside, then poked his head out as Ella made her way to Josiah. "Are we going to your friend's to pick out a puppy?"

"Yes, but he wants to keep the puppies another week before you can take your choice home."

"Aw, I was hoping he could come home with me."

Ella placed her hands on her waist. "Young man, we are not going to get a puppy until we're back in our own home."

For a few seconds Robbie pouted, then his eyes lit

up, and he grinned. "But I can choose today, and he won't be sold to someone else?"

"Yes. He'll hold him until you can take him home." Josiah began disassembling the tent.

"Even if it's weeks?"

"Yes. Now help me pack this tent up so we can go."

"I'm going in to get our lunch. We'll have a picnic out here first. I don't know about you two, but I'm starved."

While Ella strolled toward the deck, Josiah glanced over his shoulder at her. He couldn't stop thinking about Ella's past. How could a man treat his wife like that? What kind of man was he? He thought about the bullies he'd encountered in his life, and anger festered in the pit of his stomach—the same kind he'd endured while held captive.

"Josiah?"

He looked at Robbie. "Yes?"

"Can Buddy go with us? He might want to see his puppies."

"Sure."

"Does your friend have Alaskan huskies, too?"

"No. Only a couple of German shepherds right now. Why?"

"I want to be a musher in the Iditarod Race when I'm old enough."

"Maybe next spring we can see the race end in Nome." Josiah finished stuffing the tent into its bag, spying Ella heading toward them, her arms full with the food hamper, jug and blanket. "Go help your mom while I put this away."

Robbie hopped up and raced toward his mother, taking the jug from her.

"Stay, Buddy," Josiah said.

His dog's ears perked forward, and he remained still while Josiah carried the camping equipment to the storage building. Inside he paused, realizing that in a short time he'd grown accustomed to having Ella and Robbie here. He cared about them—more than he should. It would be quiet when they left.

A bark, then another one, echoed through the air. He poked his head out of the shed and saw Sadie trying to get Buddy to play. But his German shepherd stayed where he was told to. Buddy had been so good for him at a rough time in his life. The puppy would be good for Robbie, too.

"Lunch," Ella said as she spread a blanket over the grass.

Josiah's stomach rumbled, and he hurried from the storage shed. Robbie plopped down on the cover, reaching toward Buddy and scratching him behind his ears.

"Play, Buddy." Josiah sat on the blanket next to the basket.

On the other side of the food hamper, Ella removed the roast-beef sandwiches. "You have to tell him to play?"

"After I give him a working command like stay, saying *play* is my way of telling him he has free time now."

This time when Sadie barked, Buddy ran after her.

Robbie rubbed his hands together. "I can't wait until I teach my dog that."

"It takes a long time and a lot of patience to have a working relationship with a dog, especially if you want one that does search and rescue. The more we work together, the more in tune we are."

"I can do that, too."

After Ella blessed the food, Robbie grabbed a sandwich and began eating. Josiah smiled, watching the boy stuff the food into his mouth and wash it down with gulps of lemonade.

Five minutes later, Robbie jumped up. "I'm gonna play with Sadie and Buddy. I haven't thrown the tennis ball for them today."

Josiah stared at the two dogs and Robbie. "Buddy and Sadie aren't going to know what to do once your son leaves here."

"They've been good for him. Helped take his mind off Foster."

"I was talking with Alex this morning before she left for the store. She suggested camping on one of the islands. She's been wanting to try out some new equipment."

"That sounds great. I haven't gone to any of the islands off Alaska."

"I'm going to check around to see what would be fun and adventurous."

Both of her eyebrows hiked up. "Adventurous?"

"Robbie told me he wants to have an adventure. Hunt animals but not shoot them. He said he has a camera. He wants to take pictures."

"Shooting photographs, not bullets, is fine by me."

"I thought it would be a good time to teach him about being in the wilderness and how to act around the various animals."

"I could learn that, too," she said with a chuckle.

"I freaked out when I saw the bear prints in the park. You didn't. I've heard animals can smell fear."

"I'm going to make you into an outdoorswoman before this is over with. That's one of the beautiful things about Alaska. We're the last frontier in the United States." Josiah took a sip of his drink. "Have you talked to David today?"

"No. When I left the search for Seth, he told me he didn't want to hear from me until Sunday. This was my time off. He said he wouldn't answer my call."

"That sounds like him. I haven't heard yet when the postponed training session will be held."

"He wanted to wait and see if Foster is caught. I think he's worried the man will try to take another child." Ella busied herself putting the trash and bag of chips back into the food hamper. "Has Thomas called with an update?"

"Right before I came out here to demonstrate the camping equipment. And before you say anything, I was going to tell you when Robbie wasn't around." He continued when Ella looked at him, "He dumped the car he took in Girdwood and has stolen another one."

"Where?"

"South Anchorage. The police are tightening the noose, so to speak. Watching traffic cams, keeping a close eye out for any missing vehicles. I don't think it will be long before he's caught."

Ella scanned the yard, her gaze zeroing in on the woods at the back of his property. She shivered. "What if he's back there watching us right now?"

"Not possible without Buddy and Sadie knowing. They guard this property well."

"I knew I should have gotten a big dog when we first came to Anchorage. Foster would never have gotten into my backyard that night, but back then I didn't even know if I would be staying."

"No one should have to live in fear." He could remember each day he was a prisoner, wondering if it was his last one. After a while, he'd become numb to the fear.

"I've forgotten what it's like not to be afraid, but over the years the more I've learned to turn it over to the Lord, the better I've been able to handle it... except last night."

Josiah covered her hand on the food hamper handle. "With good reason. We all have moments of vulnerability."

"Robbie doesn't know most of what I told you last night. In fact, very few people do."

"He won't learn it from me. It's not my story to tell."

"What is *your* story, Josiah?"

"Boring and dull."

"Josiah, can we go now?" Robbie shouted as he tossed the tennis ball for Sadie.

"He lasted longer than I thought he would." Ella picked up the blanket and folded it.

"Let's go." Josiah carried the food hamper toward the house, thankful for Robbie's timely interruption.

Ella's son said goodbye to Sadie and ran toward the deck with Buddy at his side. "I'll get his leash."

Josiah set the basket on the kitchen counter for Linda and walked into the hallway. "I need to get my keys. Meet you two at the truck."

As he climbed the stairs, he glimpsed Robbie leading Buddy toward the kitchen. In a short time, he'd come to feel as though Ella and Robbie belonged here. He'd miss them when they returned to their own house.

More than he realized.

"Okay, David, I'll put the training session on my calendar for that Saturday." Josiah reclined in his desk chair in his home office. "Do you want me to tell Ella, or are you going to?"

"I've been avoiding talking to her. Every time I do, she asks a ton of questions about what's going on with Northern Frontier and when she can return to work." A heavy sigh came through the line. "I'll call her. I think I have an idea how she can work from your house and get most of her duties done, if you're okay with it."

"Sure. She's been talking about work more and more the past few days and keeps checking the news to see if Foster has been found. That sighting yesterday got her excited, but so far nothing has come of it. I'll keep you informed with what's happening with Ella." Josiah hated seeing disappointment on her face. She tried to hide it, especially for Robbie, but he always saw a glimpse when she didn't think anyone was looking. This was wearing her down.

He swiveled his chair around to stare out the window. Gray sheets of rain fell from the sky. It was a dreary day. Most of the time, when he wasn't working, he, Robbie and Ella were outside enjoying the outdoors. The last thing he'd taught them about camping was how to make a fire without the benefit of a lighter or matches. Robbie learned right away. Ella was a whole different story. They would starve if they depended on her to make the fire.

Suddenly his cell phone rang. He saw that it was Thomas and quickly picked it up. "I hope this is good news."

"It's about Foster."

NINE

Robbie sat in front of the window in the den with his face flat up against the glass. "Mom, it's been raining *all* day. When is it gonna stop? Buddy is bored and wants me to throw the ball for him." He spun around and grinned. "I've got an idea. What if I throw the ball down the upstairs hall? It's long and—"

Ella held her hand up. "You will *not* do that, and if you do, you'll be grounded. You think this is boring. Wait until you're by yourself the rest of the day."

He faced the window again and resumed his staring contest with the rainy day.

She wasn't going to admit to Robbie that she was bored, too. The bleak grayness reflected her mood. The rain had been falling for the past twenty-four hours. Josiah had been working a lot in his home office, which she couldn't begrudge him because he'd rearranged his life to protect her and Robbie. But she missed doing activities with him, and even talking with him. Once she'd opened up about Keith, a deluge had begun. She finally had someone to confide in. She'd felt as though she'd been released from a prison of silence.

Robbie glanced at Buddy. "I'm bored, too."

Ella pressed her lips together. All his toys and books were at their house. Maybe Josiah could take them home so Robbie could get some. She started to say something to her son when her cell phone rang.

"Hi, David. Josiah told me you had an incident you and some of the others helped with a couple of days ago. How did it turn out?"

"Two people died in a plane crash not far from Fairbanks. Pilot error. I'm calling to find out if you'd like to work from home next week or take another vacation week. I think we can set up a temporary office at Josiah and Alex's house. There are some funding reports that are due soon, but if I need to, I can explain they'll be a little late."

"No. I can get them done. You can forward calls to the main number here. It can work. I just need to ask Josiah if it's all right."

"It is. I called him a few minutes ago."

"Good." Ella looked over at what Robbie was doing. He was still at his post at the window.

"I'll come over tomorrow afternoon with what you'll need," David told her.

When Ella disconnected the call, she walked over to her son and settled her hand on his shoulder. "Hon, I think we need to get a few of your toys and games from our house. The forecast is for rain through tomorrow, if not longer."

Robbie hugged her. "That would be great! Do you think Josiah would be okay with it?"

Just then, Josiah came into the den and Buddy greeted him. "Yes, I am. We should have done that in the beginning. Especially for days like this when I'm stuck working and the weather isn't cooperating."

Her son punched the air. "Yes!"

Josiah smiled at Robbie. "We'll leave in a minute. Linda told me she needed a cookie taster. Do you want the job?"

"What kind?"

"Chocolate chip."

"I can do it," Robbie said as he raced from the room with Buddy on his heels.

Ella drew in a deep breath. "Nothing beats that smell. I may have to apply to be Linda's taster, too."

"Before you do, I have something to tell you about Foster."

"You talked with Thomas?"

He nodded. "Last night Foster was spotted at Big Lake by a man who tried to stop him. Foster knocked the guy out, then tied him up. By the time the man was found and reported it, Foster had been gone for twelve hours. They suspect he's heading into the backcountry."

"So he somehow made his way from Girdwood to Big Lake unseen by the authorities."

"The vehicle he was last reported driving has been found. They aren't sure what he's driving now."

She hadn't prepared herself enough for the fact that Foster might never be caught. She couldn't stay at the estate forever. Maybe she would have to leave Alaska and the friends she'd made, not because of her ex-husband, but because of Foster. She didn't want to feel like a prisoner again and certainly didn't wa it for her son.

"From the encounter at Big Lake, the police

know Foster has altered his appearance, and has sent out an updated sketch as well as possible variations."

"What does he look like now?"

"Here." Josiah gave her his cell phone.

"Blond hair cut short, no beard, glasses." She could remember when she'd changed her appearance to get away from Keith. It had worked. She prayed Foster's new look didn't work as well for him.

"Mom, can we go now?" Robbie entered the den with a half-eaten chocolate-chip cookie in his hand.

Josiah turned toward her son. "Yes. I'm finished for the day. You'll have to show me your stuff."

"Can I bring it all?"

"Robbie! We are not packing up your room to bring here. You get to pick five or six things you want."

"Mom, that isn't much. It'll be hard to decide."

"But I'm confident you'll be able to do it."

Robbie pouted. "I'm glad you are. I'm not."

Josiah clasped his shoulder. "I'll help. Let's go. Linda said dinner would be ready in an hour."

"And she let Robbie have some cookies?"

"Only one," Robbie said and popped the last bit into his mouth. "She told me I could have more later." He headed toward the garage off the kitchen. "Can Buddy come, too?"

Ella followed her son with Josiah a few steps behind her. "Buddy has been with you every waking moment today. Let's give him time to rest." There was no way the dog had been getting his usual amount of sleep.

Fifteen minutes later, Josiah pulled into her drive-y. She hadn't been home for over a week. "Remember, no more than six items. We aren't moving into the estate, just visiting. And we don't have a lot of time."

"Yeah. Alex has a date." Josiah climbed from his truck.

Curious, Ella hopped from the cab and hurried after Josiah. "With who? I didn't know she was dating anyone."

Josiah chuckled. "Neither did I. Honestly, I think this is a business date." While Robbie ran ahead to the porch, he leaned close to Ella and whispered, "Trust me. She isn't serious. She prefers being single."

"I certainly understand that." Ella dug into her purse and withdrew her key, then opened the front door.

Josiah clasped her arm, stopping her from going inside, while Robbie darted across the threshold. "Not all men are like your ex-husband. Alex was happily married for five years."

"I'm glad," Ella responded, then she turned and called out to Robbie, "Wait up."

Josiah moved past Ella and Robbie. "Let me do a quick walk-through first."

Her son scuffed his tennis shoes against the floor while Josiah checked the house. When the sound of Josiah's footsteps returning to the foyer indicated he'd finished, Robbie ran toward the hallway, leading to the bedrooms.

"He's done. I need all my time to make some serious decisions about what I'm gonna take." Passing Josiah, Robbie disappeared around the corner.

"If I don't supervise, he'll manage somehow to bring his whole toy chest. His school backpack is hanging on a peg in the garage." She heard a slamming sound coming from Robbie's room. "Will you get it while I corral my son?"

"Yeah, sure."

Something else thumped to the floor. She hurried to his bedroom. When she stepped into the entrance, he was looking through a drawer and suddenly plucked a set of action figures out of it then tossed them on the bed.

"That's one." Robbie went to his closet and started to open it.

"That's seven action figures. That's seven items, so…" Something was wrong here. The overhead light was on. She shifted her attention to the window with the blackout shade pulled down. She hadn't left it that way. Quickly she pulled it up. Her gaze widened at the sight of the window ajar a few inches. "Don't open the closet."

Josiah walked through the living room and dining room into the kitchen. He paused at the sink window and looked outside. The rain had let up as they drove here, but now it was starting to come down hard again. He continued his trek to the garage and stepped down into it. Ella's black Jeep Wrangler was parked close to the door, but on the other side was a white Honda.

The hairs on the back of his neck stood up. He pivoted toward the house. Something solid came down on his head. He crumpled to the concrete floor.

As Robbie flung his closet door open, he swiveled around. "Why not? Some of my favorite toys are in there."

Expecting someone to come charging out, Ella frantically searched for something to use as a weapon. When no one came out, with Robbie's baseball bat in hand, she whispered, "Get behind me," then inched forward.

Using the wooden stick, she poked behind the clothes hanging up. "Robbie, did you open your window and forget to close it?" She came out of the closet.

His wide gaze riveted to her. He shook his head, the color washing from his face.

"Stay behind me. Someone might be in the house."

"But Josiah checked each room."

He wouldn't have seen the open window because the shade was pulled down. Her shaky hand withdrew her cell phone from her pocket. She found Thomas's number and punched it as she crept down the hall to the bathroom. "Thomas, this is Ella. Josiah brought us to our house to get some toys. I think someone has been here. May still be here." Her whispery voice rasped from her throat.

"Where's Josiah?"

"In the garage." Ella checked behind the shower curtain in the bathroom.

"Get him and get out of there. I'm on my way."

As she hung up, a crashing sound came from the garage reverberating through the house. Josiah! If she could get to her purse on the hallway table, she could get her gun.

"Robbie, lock the bathroom door and don't open it unless it's me or Josiah. Okay?"

Fear filled his face. He nodded.

"You'll be all right. The police are on their way." She waited a couple of heartbeats until her son clicked the lock in place, then she snuck toward the foyer to get her Glock. One of the first things she'd done after she'd left her husband was learn to shoot a gun to protect herself.

A large man, his back to Josiah, headed for the door into the house. Josiah fought to keep conscious. If he didn't, Robbie would be kidnapped. He didn't want him to be taken prisoner. Flashes of his own captivity swamped him for a few seconds. He shut down his emotions and went into combat mode.

He struggled to his feet, steadying himself while looking around for a weapon. There was nothing within reach. With his head pounding, he moved forward as the large man glanced over his shoulder at him.

Foster spun around and came toward him like the grizzly Robbie had called him. Josiah charged the man, ramming his left shoulder into Foster's chest. He slammed back against the wall, the shuddering sound resonating like a shock wave through the garage. The man wound his arm around Josiah and squeezed. His breath leaving his lungs, he kicked Foster, then kneed him as Josiah wrestled to loosen the arms about his torso. Again he struck Foster with the toe of his boot.

The hulking man shoved away from the wall and drove Josiah into Ella's car, swooshing out what little air remained in his lungs. Trapped between the hood and Foster, Josiah pounded his fists into the man's back, gasping for oxygen. Dizziness sapped what strength he had left.

The sounds of fighting coming from the garage sent Ella's heartbeat racing as she neared the open door. With sweaty hands, she held a baseball bat in one hand and her gun in the other. At the threshold she peered around the door frame while preparing to help Josiah. Foster outweighed him by at least fifty pounds from the pictures she'd seen of the man.

Her heartbeat thudded against her rib cage as she spied Foster pinning Josiah against her car. Crushing him.

She had to do something, but she couldn't shoot Foster. She might hit Josiah, too. Fortifying herself with a deep breath, she laid her gun on the counter nearby and gripped the baseball bat with both hands.

The police are on the way. I can do this.

She crept toward the pair and raised the bat.

Foster looked back, his dark eyes boring into her. He started to turn toward her.

She brought the bat down on his shoulder. The first blow stunned him, but he kept turning. She swung the bat again, connecting with the side of his head. The hulk teetered for a few seconds, then collapsed to the floor.

She hurried to Josiah. Drawing in deep gulps of air, he slid down the side of the car.

He reached toward Foster and felt for a pulse. "He's alive. You need to call the police."

"I already did. How do you feel?"

"I think he cracked a rib. Robbie had it right. He's like a grizzly bear even without all the facial hair he used to have." With each breath, Josiah winced.

Ella gave him the bat. "Hit him if he moves. I left my gun in the kitchen."

She hurried inside, snatched it from the counter

and returned to the garage. The sight of the pain on Josiah's face tore at her. "I'm calling an ambulance."

"No. I've had worse injuries. After the police leave, we'll go to the emergency room, but I'm not leaving you and Robbie until Foster is hauled away." Laying the bat on the floor, he held out his hand. "I'll trade you."

"I know how to shoot," she said as she passed him the gun. "But I'm not going to argue with an injured man."

"Where's Robbie?"

"Locked in the bathroom."

The sight of red lights flashing across the walls prompted Ella to push the button to raise the garage door.

"I'll take care of this. Go check on Robbie." Josiah pushed to his feet using the car as support.

Ella spied Thomas walking up the driveway. She hurried into the house to let Robbie know everything was all right and to make sure he didn't see Foster. The man had already traumatized her son enough.

"Robbie, this is Mom. You can come out now."

The lock clicked, and Robbie swung the door wide and rushed into her arms. "I was so scared. I…" Sobs drowned out the rest of his words.

She hugged him to her. When he quieted, she knelt and clasped his arm. "Honey, the police will take Foster away. We're safe. And so is Josiah. We have no reason to be afraid anymore."

Tears ran down his cheeks unchecked. "I didn't know—" he gasped for air "—what was going on."

"Foster attacked Josiah in the garage. He must have

been out there waiting. The important part is that he'll be put away for a long time."

"Where Josiah?"

"He's with the police, but you and I are going to sit in the living room and wait until Foster is hauled away. I'm sure the police will want to talk to both of us."

"Foster wasn't in the house?"

"No, the garage." She didn't want him to know that Foster had parked a car in the garage or that in all likelihood he'd been in their house—maybe for hours. She'd have to deal with that, but she didn't want Robbie to.

"But my window was opened?"

She wouldn't lie to her son, but she would try to play down the fact he was inside at some time. "Yes. He might have gotten in that way or another way. We'll let the police figure that out. Let's concentrate on the fact he has finally been caught and we can return home."

"I don't want to," Robbie cried out and ran into the bathroom, locking the door.

"Honey, open up please." She tried turning the knob, hoping she was wrong about the lock. She wasn't.

"Go away. I'm safe in here."

Looking up and down the hallway produced no great ideas of how to get her son out of the bathroom. There was a part of her that wanted to hide in there with him. "Please, sweetie. You're safe now. Come out."

Out of the corner of her eye, she glimpsed movement and reacted. Hands fisted, she rotated as though she would stop anyone from getting to her son. When she saw it was Josiah and Thomas, she sank against the door. The trembling started in her fingers and quickly spread throughout her body.

Josiah strode to her and started to pull her to him. "Okay?"

Remembering his ribs, she sidled away. "I'm okay. You aren't. I need to get you to the hospital."

"Not until I know Robbie is all right. Let me talk to him while Thomas interviews you."

"Thanks." She moved away while Josiah knocked on the door.

"Robbie, this is Josiah. Can I come in and talk to you?"

Ella walked toward Thomas at the end of the hall, praying that Robbie would let Josiah in.

Silence ruled for a long moment.

"Robbie, I'll only stay as long as you want." Josiah's voice softened, conveying concern.

Her son unlocked the door and slowly opened it. Ella stepped out of view. She'd wanted to be the one who comforted her child, but if she couldn't, then she thanked the Lord Josiah was here to help Robbie deal with everything.

Thomas touched her elbow, drawing her attention to him. "Let's go in the living room. This whole situation has been tough for Robbie, but also for you, Ella."

She hugged her arms to her chest and followed Thomas. When she sank onto the couch, the police detective sat in a chair across from her. In the distance she heard a siren. "Is that an ambulance for Foster?"

"Yes. While I was in the garage, he regained consciousness but was groggy. Don't worry. A team of police officers will be guarding him until we get him to the jail. He won't get away from us. I promise." Controlled anger hardened his voice. "He won't terrorize you or any other families again."

As her adrenaline subsided, a chill gave her goose bumps from the top of her head to her toes. "I knew something was wrong when I saw Robbie's blackout shade down and his window cracked open. Now that I think about it, the bed was rumpled." She shivered, picturing Foster lying on it, waiting for her son. "What if he'd been in the closet rather than the garage? Josiah had a hard time fighting him off. I can't imagine me trying."

"You stopped him, though, with quick and calm thinking. Why don't you tell me everything from when you arrived at the house?"

Ella peered toward the hallway, then started from the beginning, but the whole time her thoughts dwelled on Robbie and Josiah in the bathroom.

Robbie sat on the edge of the bathtub while Josiah leaned against the counter across from him, wincing when he moved the wrong way and a stab of pain pierced his chest. The boy stared at the tile floor, his hands gripping the tub edge so tightly his fingertips were red.

"I watched the police take Foster away. He can't hurt you, partner."

Ella's son didn't look up or say a word.

Not sure exactly how to comfort the child, Josiah cleared his throat. He'd had little interaction with kids in the past. He plowed his fingers through his hair, trying to think of something to say that would help Robbie.

"You and your mom are safe now."

The boy lifted his head, his eyes shiny with unshed tears.

"I promise."

"He...he was in my...house." Robbie shuddered.

Josiah squatted in front of the child. "He isn't now and won't be in the future. He'll go to prison for a long time."

"He scared Mom."

"I know, but she's all right. You saw her."

"He scared Mom like my..." Robbie's eyes widened, and he clamped his hand over his mouth.

Dad? Given what Ella had told him about her ex-husband, Robbie had probably been schooled not to say a word about his past. "But you two are all right now. That's what is important."

"But I was so scared. I was a crybaby. I need to be big and strong for Mom."

"There's nothing wrong with being afraid. Fear is an emotion we have to help us deal with certain situations. I've known people who were fearless, and they ended up hurting themselves and others. Fear makes us consider all possible answers to a problem, then hopefully we pick the best solution rather than just reacting."

"Have you ever been afraid?"

"Yes. I was today. I didn't want Foster to hurt you or your mom."

Robbie straightened. "He's a bad man."

"He's done some bad things, and he will pay for that. There are consequences to our actions."

"Like when me and my friends left camp when we weren't supposed to?"

Josiah nodded. "Are you ready to go see your mom now? She's worried about you."

"Yes."

Josiah put his hand on the edge of the counter and struggled to his feet. The sharp pain sliced through his chest. He needed to go to the hospital.

But at least he'd reassured Robbie that he was safe.

TEN

"Mom, is Josiah gonna hafta stay in the hospital tonight?" Robbie looked up from the paper he was drawing on in the waiting room of the emergency room.

"I don't know. We should hear something soon." Ella's gaze strayed to the entrance, as it had so often done in the past hour since Josiah had been taken to see a doctor. The minutes since then had passed agonizingly slowly. He was hurt because of her. She knew how painful a broken or even cracked rib could be.

"How come Alex isn't here?"

"Josiah made me promise not to call her, but if he's admitted, I will."

"You can't break a promise to him."

"Okay, you're right. I'll make sure he calls his sister. She needs to know if he's in the hospital."

"And Buddy."

She smiled. "Yeah, Buddy, too."

Robbie went back to making a picture for Josiah while she kept looking toward the doorway. Worry twisted her stomach into knots.

Ten minutes later, Josiah appeared in the doorway, looking worn out but relieved. One corner of his mouth lifted. "Ready to get out of here?"

Robbie jumped to his feet, grabbed his work of art and rushed to Josiah. "I made you a picture."

While he looked at the drawing, she bridged the distance between them. "He's been working the past half hour on it."

He tousled her son's hair. "You never told me you could draw like this. Buddy is going to love this."

"I was afraid you'd hafta stay here and you wouldn't get to see Buddy."

"Let me see." Ella stepped next to Josiah. "He wouldn't show me while he was working."

Josiah held a picture of him with Buddy sitting beside him.

"I still have to put in a few more trees. It's a drawing of you at Kincaid Park."

"Tell you what. I'll loan it to you to finish, but I want it back when you're through." Josiah's voice grew huskier as he spoke. "No one has ever made me a gift like that." He swallowed hard. "Let's go. I hate hospitals."

"Me, too." Robbie took Josiah's hand. "I had to visit Mom in the hospital once, and it scared me."

On the other side of Josiah, Ella leaned forward. "Robbie, they fixed me up. Just like they did Josiah. You love visiting Bree at the clinic. Hospitals are just bigger clinics."

Outside Ella stopped. "You two stay here. I'll bring your truck around."

"I can walk—"

She narrowed her gaze on him, halting Josiah's

words. "Let me take care of you for once. Keys, please." She held out her palm flat.

"Yes, ma'am." He tossed her the keys to the F-150. "Just remember a man and his truck have a special bond."

She laughed as she left Josiah and Robbie at the entrance to the emergency room. With the capture of Foster, she felt a weight lifted from her shoulders. No more hiding. No more watching over her shoulder.

Twenty minutes later, she drove the truck into the garage at Josiah's estate. She glanced over at him, the side of his head resting against the passenger window, his eyelids half-closed. "Home sweet home."

"Buddy's probably worried. I'll let him know you're okay." Robbie climbed from the backseat and headed for the door into the house.

"Josiah, do you need me to help you inside?"

He perked up. "No, I can make it on my own. They gave me something for the pain, and I believe it's starting to take effect."

"Good. You need rest."

"Will you do me a favor?"

"Yes, of course."

"Don't go home until tomorrow. I think it would be a good thing if Robbie had Buddy with him when he goes back home for the first time after Foster was caught."

"Sure. It's late anyway, and per your request I didn't tell Alex about your being hurt. Before we go inside, tell me what the doctor said about your injuries."

"A couple of bruised ribs and a knot on my head. Time will take care of everything. I'll be fine soon."

"Yeah, you're one tough guy. It's okay to admit it hurts."

"Was Keith the reason you were in the hospital?"

"Oh, no, you don't. Today is about you and your injuries. Not mine. I'm not going to talk about my past right now."

"I respect that." Josiah glanced toward the house. "I think your son is waiting for us to come in."

Sitting next to Robbie, Buddy barked.

"I think your dog needs to make sure you're all right." Ella opened the driver's door, hopped down and started to round the hood to help Josiah whether he wanted it or not. She owed him so much.

But he eased out of the cab before she could get to him, a grimace on his face.

"I think I remember someone I know telling me it's okay to accept help." Ella closed the space between them.

"I'm putting up a brave front for Robbie and Buddy."

"Sure." She walked next to Josiah and watched as he put on a brave front—no doubt for Robbie. She'd done that herself in the past.

At the door, Robbie stepped to the side to let them into the house. "Buddy missed me badly. So did Sadie."

"Let's go upstairs. You need to rest," Ella said to Josiah, proceeding through the kitchen toward the foyer. "Now that you're home, can I tell Alex, Linda and Harry what happened to you?"

"Yes, I can't hide much from Alex. The twin thing."

"Is there really something to that?"

"Yup, at least with me and Alex there is."

Robbie and Buddy followed behind them to the second floor.

At his bedroom door, Josiah turned toward them. "I'm okay. I'm going to bed. I don't need a nurse."

Ella frowned. He didn't see his face each time a certain movement caused him pain.

Josiah's eyes softened. "I'll be fine. Promise." He opened his door and started inside.

"Wait," Robbie said. "You need Buddy tonight. I don't. Foster has been caught." Robbie waved his hand toward the room. "Go, Buddy."

When Buddy didn't follow the command, Josiah ruffled Robbie's hair. "Thanks." Then to his German shepherd, he said, "Come."

When the bedroom door shut, Ella placed her hand on her son's shoulder. "That must have been hard for you."

"Yup, but Buddy is his dog." He stood up taller. "I'm fine. Josiah isn't."

"It's past your bedtime. You need to get your sleep, too. Tomorrow we go back home and get our normal lives back."

"But I don't want to leave."

"You'll get your own dog soon and be busy taking care of him."

Robbie's face brightened. "And training him. When can I go get him?"

"Maybe sometime next week. I'll be in to say good-night in a few moments."

Ella slipped inside her bedroom and sank onto the bed, the day's events flooding her mind finally. She'd

managed to hold them at bay while talking to the police and making sure Josiah was all right, but now the
implications of what had occurred earlier deluged her.
Her body shook. She hugged herself trying to control the tremors rocking her, but it didn't stop them.

Today could have ended so badly.

*Thank You, Lord. Without You, I couldn't have
done half the things I've had to do these past four
years.*

While watching Robbie play with Buddy and
Sadie in the backyard, Ella sipped her coffee on Josiah and Alex's deck. Earlier she'd called David and
let him know she was returning to work the next
day. He'd already heard from Thomas about what
had happened at her house. She was glad she didn't
have to go into details. She just wanted to put Foster
behind her and move on. Today she'd need to find a
place for Robbie to stay while she was at the Northern Frontier office.

The sound of footsteps invaded her thoughts.

Alex sat in the chair next to her. "I really need this
coffee. Thanks for putting a note on my bedroom door
about Josiah. I should wring his neck for keeping the
fact he went to the hospital from me."

"I tried to convince him I should call you. But he
wanted you to enjoy yourself since there really wasn't
anything you could do."

"Sometimes my brother exasperates me."

"Just sometimes?"

Alex laughed. "He keeps hoping I'll meet another
man and marry again. That isn't going to happen. I

had a beautiful marriage and five glorious years. I don't see anyone taking my husband's place. He may be gone, but he still lives in my heart."

Ella had wanted that so much and had thought Keith was the man for her. Now she felt the same way Alex did about marrying again, but for the opposite reason. "You don't get lonely?"

"No. I have friends and my business. Those keep me busy. I don't have time for a man. How about you?"

"I have all those things and my son. I have a fulfilling life." But as Ella said that, something was different than before. She hadn't gotten to know Josiah until recently. Even if he could make her forget the nightmare of her marriage, she didn't plan to make the same mistake twice. She hoped Josiah and her could be good friends. He was wonderful for Robbie. But anything beyond that wasn't possible.

"I'm going to miss you two after today. I've enjoyed getting to know you. And I know Josiah has. You've made him laugh and smile more than I've seen in a long time."

"Did something happen to him?" Ella stopped herself from asking anything further. If she ever learned about his past, he should be the one to tell her. She knew little about him other than that he grew up in Alaska. There were too many years unaccounted for before and after he was a US Marine.

"He doesn't talk about it."

"I can understand. The past is the past."

"I like you a lot. I hope one day he'll share his past with you."

Her curiosity was aroused. Just because she'd

shared her past completely with him didn't mean he had to do so, but she'd hoped he would trust her enough to confide in her.

"I hope you two aren't conspiring." Josiah, dressed in jeans and a long-sleeved T-shirt, joined them and took the seat on the other side of Ella.

"Yes, because you've been a bad brother. Next time you go to the emergency room, you better call me or have someone else let me know. If you don't, you're going to rue the day you made that decision." Her voice was calm and quiet, yet as Alex sipped her coffee, her gaze drilled into Josiah.

"I tried to tell him yesterday." Ella shot him a look of satisfaction.

"I see. You are ganging up on me. I'm injured. I need your sympathy." A twinkle danced in his eyes as he carefully leaned back in the lounger, his legs stretched out in front of him.

Robbie raced toward the deck with the two dogs close by. "You're up. How are you?"

Josiah threw Ella and Alex an irritated glance. "At least Robbie cares. Yes, I'm okay."

"Great. Then you can come show me some more commands. I'm getting my puppy this week."

"That's good. I'll be out there in a sec."

Robbie ran back to the middle of the yard and flung the Frisbee for Buddy while Josiah struggled out of his lounger. He winced.

"It's okay to admit you're in pain." Ella hated seeing him like that.

"Nope. I'm not letting it get the best of me. Life goes on."

Slowly Josiah made his way toward her son.

"That's his motto. Mind over matter."

"Has he been injured a lot?"

Alex's forehead scrunched. "Yes, but he doesn't talk about it."

Ella watched him interact with Robbie. She and Josiah were similar in a lot of ways—even about keeping secrets.

"Are you sure you don't want me to leave Buddy here tonight?" Josiah sat on Ella's couch with his German shepherd at his feet later that evening.

She settled next to Josiah. "Robbie slept without him last night at your house. He should be okay. We're going after work on Wednesday to get the puppy he picked out."

"Does he have a name for him yet?"

"Sam."

"Where did that name come from?"

"He didn't know. It just popped into his head when he saw him at the breeder's house last week."

"Is everything set for you going back to work tomorrow?"

"Yes. My neighbor will watch him for me. I loved staying at your place and we both know Robbie did, but it feels good to be home and back to my normal life."

"The vacation is over," Josiah said with a chuckle.

"If the past week was a vacation, I never want to go on another one. Loved the company but not the reason for being there."

Josiah sobered. "Yeah, a normal life is good, but I still owe Robbie a camping trip."

"That would be nice. Now, that would be a real vacation without a lunatic coming after us."

"That's what I was thinking. I already have one of the islands picked out."

She clasped his hand and cupped it between hers. "You don't have to. Robbie and I have taken up too much of your time." She needed to put some distance between them before she fell in love with him. *I have to listen to my head, not my heart.*

"First, I want to. Second, I promised Robbie and third, I enjoy camping and sharing the experience with others. I've even persuaded Alex to take some time off from work, which is a feat in itself, to join us."

Ella rubbed her fingers across the back of his hand. "What about your injuries?"

"We'll wait until they're better. Thankfully my threshold for pain is high."

"I'm just glad you were here when Foster decided to hide out in my house." She refused to think what would have happened if he hadn't been there.

"So is Thomas. He called today to tell me we've made his life a little easier with the capture of Foster."

"It's always nice to accommodate the police. Although I can't believe Foster had the nerve to use my home as a hideout."

"He figured you weren't coming back as long as he was loose."

"How do you know that?"

"He told Thomas." Josiah rose slowly and carefully. "I'd better go. You have to get up early. You've been a woman of leisure for the past week, and it may take you a while to get used to your work routine again. Do you have someone to watch Robbie beyond tomorrow?"

"Yes, my neighbor insisted she would since she and her husband are back from their three-week trek through Alaska. Both of my neighbors on each side have been a good support system for me."

"Good." He headed for the front door.

Ella went out on the porch with him as the sun was starting to go down. "Thank you again for your help. With everything."

He turned toward her, a smile dimpling his cheeks. "My pleasure. We'll talk before you go to pick up Sam. I'd like to go with you." He inched closer.

"I'd like that." She tilted up her chin, so close to Josiah she could smell mint on his breath. She lifted her hand and cradled his cheek, wanting him to kiss her and yet hesitating to make the first move.

He bent toward her, his lips softly capturing hers. Then he pulled back. "I'd better leave."

No, don't. But she wouldn't say it out loud because he was right. It was better that he left now. She didn't know what to do about the feelings swirling around in her head concerning Josiah. She needed some space between them until she figured out how to be a friend and nothing more.

"Yes, you're right. Talk to you this week."

She waited on the porch until he drove away, thinking back to all that had occurred recently. Josiah had always been there in the center of the action. In that short time she'd become dependent on him. She'd vowed she would never feel that way about a man again. She wasn't a risk taker, although everything in her shouted that Josiah wasn't a risk.

She shook her head, trying to empty her thoughts of him. But she wasn't successful.

With a deep sigh, she pushed open the front door.

To find her son standing in the foyer looking into the living room, fear on his face.

He whirled around and flew at her. "I thought you'd left me alone or something."

"No, honey. I was saying goodbye to Josiah on the porch. Is something wrong?"

"I can't sleep. I tried really hard, Mom." His eyes filled with tears, and he bit his lower lip.

"That's okay. Sometimes it takes a while to fall asleep."

A tear ran down his face. "I'm scared. What if Foster escapes from jail?"

She smoothed his hair off his forehead. "He won't."

"He was in my bedroom."

"We don't know that for sure." Although she thought he had been, she didn't want to confirm it for Robbie.

"He must have opened my window. I didn't. You didn't."

"Well, he can't now. He has police officers guarding him, and he's behind bars."

"I miss Buddy. He made me feel safe."

"He wasn't with you last night."

"That's because Josiah needed him more, and I felt safe at his house."

"You love this house, and your room."

"I want to move to the other bedroom."

"It's smaller."

"I don't care. That man ruined my room for me."

Sadness enveloped Ella, and she wished she

could turn back time. *Lord, please help Robbie. He shouldn't have to feel this fear at his age.*

"Will you sit with me while I fall asleep?"

"Of course."

He hugged her. "You're the best."

A few minutes later, Ella sat against the headboard in Robbie's room with her son cuddled up against her. For the first half hour, his eyes kept popping open to check she was still there. Then the next thirty minutes, they stayed closed, but her son twisted and turned. By the second hour, he finally calmed, and soon he fell asleep.

But Ella was wide-awake with no hope of going to bed anytime soon. Darkness shrouded her, and if it wouldn't have awakened her son, she would have turned on a light. She didn't want to take that chance. Like her son, she'd slept well at Josiah's. Now every sound outside spiked her heartbeat. Even staring at the window, she imagined Foster crawling through it and snatching Robbie from her arms.

With thoughts of Keith, it had taken her over a year in Anchorage before she'd gotten a good night's sleep. She was determined Foster wouldn't invade her peace—her son's. She searched her mind for something to think about that brought a feeling of safety, calm.

Josiah.

No doubt about it. She'd never met someone quite like him. She could talk to him about things she didn't with others. That still amazed her.

But a big part of his life was a mystery to her. He held a large part of himself back. She could never allow her heart to become involved. Could she?

* * *

Josiah sat at his desk in his home office. "I'll bring Buddy over this evening. He can stay the next two nights until you take Sam home. Do you think that will help Robbie sleep?"

"Thank you, Josiah. Are you sure?"

Hearing the relief in Ella's voice confirmed his decision, even though he'd awakened last night in a cold sweat. "Yes. It's only for a couple of nights. I'll be fine. Remember, you two had Buddy before." If he wasn't, he'd deal with it. He didn't want Robbie becoming so scared he couldn't sleep.

"You're a lifesaver, and I know Robbie will be thrilled. At least let me treat you to a dinner. I hope you'll be able to stay when you drop Buddy off."

"I'll make time in my busy schedule," Josiah said with a chuckle. "Since the doctor told me to rest and take it easy for two or three days, I've been working from home."

"Good thing you have an understanding boss. See you later."

After he hung up, Josiah leaned back in his chair and stared out the window at his backyard. Serene. Peaceful. And yet inside, he couldn't shake the memories of Foster's heavy weight pressing down on him, squeezing all the air from his lungs. The sensation of not being able to breathe had thrown him back to his time as a POW. The past two nights, his nightmares had returned, and Buddy had been there to wake him from the horrors he relived.

A tightness in his chest that had nothing to do with his bruised ribs spread. Before he could call Buddy, his German shepherd was in front of him, nudging his hand. Taking breaths as deep as was possible, he stroked his dog, thinking of his present life. Ella. Robbie. Slowly his panic subsided.

But would it tonight, without Buddy?

ELEVEN

Thursday evening, Ella inhaled a deep breath of the outdoorsy scent of the Russian Jack Springs Park. "It was a good idea to walk Buddy and Sam together. Sam is already responding to Buddy, and he's a great role model for our puppy."

"How was your first night with Sam?" Josiah walked beside her on the trail while Robbie held both leashes.

"Robbie insisted on Sam sleeping in his bed, and somehow there wasn't one accident—at least last night."

"So Robbie slept all right without Buddy?"

"Yes and thanks for the use of Buddy for a couple of nights." She slanted her head and assessed Josiah. He didn't look as tired today. Yesterday she'd wondered if he'd been getting the rest the doctor recommended. "How have you been sleeping with the bruised ribs?"

"When the doc told me to sleep on the side that's bruised, I thought he was crazy. But believe it or not, it actually is much better."

He didn't exactly answer her question, so she said,

"I'm glad you're getting the rest he said would help you get better, because my son has already started bugging me about the camping trip."

"I'm adjusting, and over-the-counter pain meds are all I have to take now. I think we could look at the first weekend in August. That's only a couple of weeks away. I know how it is when you're a child and want to do something badly, but Sam should take his focus away. I'll come over after work and help him with the puppy."

"That'll be great. I appreciate it, and so does Robbie. You and Buddy are all he talks about." But what would happen to Josiah and Robbie's relationship if another woman entered his life? He deserved to be married and be a father. He was fantastic with her son.

"Is he going to be at the training session this weekend or staying with your neighbor?"

"He wants to be at the session, but this Saturday is all business for Northern Frontier. Now that it's safe, I need to focus on my job or David might fire me."

Josiah tossed his head back and laughed. "Are you kidding? He knows a great office manager when he sees one. You should hear him rave about you."

A blush heated her cheeks. "Enough, or I might get a big head and grow right out of my ball cap."

Josiah stopped on the path while Robbie let the dogs sniff a tree off the trail. "That's just it. You don't realize how good you are. Efficient. Caring. More organized than most people. Great with people. You remind me a lot of my sister."

She was growing uncomfortable with all his compliments and needed to change the subject fast. "Is she able to come camping with us?"

"Yes, I'm sure."

"Good, because I like her a lot, and it'll give us more time to get to know each other."

"She's looking forward to it. Our love of camping as children is the reason we didn't sell Outdoor Alaska when our parents died. So it'll be good to get back to our roots. This camping trip will help us to see what new products work or don't."

"So this is a business trip?" The corners of her mouth twitched with the grin she was trying to contain.

"Not really. Not even for Alex. As much as she's a workaholic, she still sees the value in taking some time off."

"But you're not a workaholic?"

"Not like Alex. She's a diehard."

"I'm glad you aren't. There's more to life than just work."

"Believe me. I discovered that the hard…" His voice faded into silence. "We better catch up with Robbie. Sometimes it's hard to control two dogs at the same time."

Frustrated, she chewed on her bottom lip. She wanted to shout at Josiah, *Let me in!* Finally she stopped and blocked him on the path. "Why didn't you finish what you were saying?"

"Because I don't share my life with anyone. Some things are best left in the past." He skirted around her and increased his pace to catch up with Robbie.

At that moment, she realized he'd never really share his life with her. If it weren't for Robbie, she would put some distance between her and Josiah right away before she became even more invested in him. But it would break her son's heart. He'd never had a good male role model, and Josiah was quickly taking that position in Robbie's life.

That realization made her decide that after the camping trip she would have to find other role models for her son. Maybe through the Big Brothers program. She was afraid when Josiah moved on in his life, it would devastate Robbie.

"Mom, what's keeping you? I want to play on the playground before we leave."

There was no easy solution to her dilemma concerning Josiah and Robbie. She exhaled slowly. "I'm coming."

Ella came into the kitchen from her backyard and noticed Robbie hanging the phone up. "Who was that?"

He shrugged. "Wrong number, I guess."

"Josiah will be here soon. After Sam's training, we're going to Outdoor Alaska to get the camping equipment we need, so remember not to get dirty."

"Hurray! We leave in two days, and I need to practice putting up our tent."

"Only when I'm watching." She couldn't afford to buy a second tent if he ruined the first one.

"Sure, Mom. I wish you'd quit babying me. I know what I'm doing. Josiah taught me, remember?"

"True, but that was a couple of weeks ago." She'd tried to stay away from Josiah as much as possible when he came to help Robbie, but it wasn't easy when she saw him being more of a father than Keith had ever been.

"Mom, why can't Sam go with us?"

"We aren't taking the dogs. Linda and Harry will watch Sam. He'll have fun with Buddy and Sadie. I don't want to have to worry about your puppy when what we're doing is new to us."

"We're gonna be on an island. Sam couldn't go too far without meeting the Gulf of Alaska."

"What if we run into a bear? Do you want to worry about Sam doing something to get himself hurt?"

"Bears? I hadn't thought of that. Are there going to be many?"

"It's Alaska. The possibility of a bear encounter is part of living here. Remember that time the moose came down into our yard during the winter and ate our bushes? We live in a big city. That didn't stop the moose."

Robbie giggled. "I doubt much could stop a moose or a bear."

"It would take a lot. That's why you never confront one."

The doorbell chimes resonated through the house.

"That's Josiah. I'll get it," Robbie said as he rushed from the kitchen.

"Check before you open the door," she called after her son, but she doubted he heard her because two seconds later he admitted Josiah into the house, then began telling him about his day.

Ella smiled. Poor Josiah. Sometimes he couldn't get two words in.

When Josiah entered the kitchen with Robbie, he smiled at her, which sent goose bumps up and down her arms. "How was your day?"

"Fine. Just wrapping up the information about

the search and rescue of a tourist in Katmai National Park."

"From what I heard, you all did good yesterday."

Robbie looked at Josiah. "Why didn't you go with Buddy?"

"The area where the tourist disappeared has a lot of bears. In the summer they are all over Brooks Camp and the surrounding area. Dogs and bears don't mix, and they prefer that K-9s not be used in the search, at least initially. The personnel working SAR missions will vary depending on where the person went missing and who the person is."

"Sam and I are ready." Robbie started for the kitchen door.

"Good. I'll be out back in a second." When her son left, Josiah moved to her. "Are we still on for the camping trip this weekend? I know Northern Frontier has been extra busy lately."

"That's normal for a summer with so many tourists around. Robbie is counting down the hours until we leave. David has insisted I go and not to worry about Northern Frontier. There are a lot of people who can step in temporarily. Do you still want to go?" Most of the searches were outside of Anchorage, and when that happened, she manned the phones at the office, coordinating and supporting David and the searchers. With her gone a lot because of her job, she hadn't seen Josiah as much as Robbie had. Josiah had ended up helping Robbie with the puppy at her neighbor's a few times.

Josiah stared out the window at her son playing with Sam. "Most definitely. Robbie is like a sponge.

So eager to learn everything. His enthusiasm is contagious. It's good to be around him."

"Then it's still a go. Friday we leave."

Josiah went out to the backyard to start the puppy training. She stood at the sink and watched him and Robbie training Sam to obey simple commands. Her heart swelled at the sight. Robbie should have a father who cared about him.

Toward the end of the lesson, Ella went outside to remind them they still needed to go shopping at Outdoor Alaska.

As Josiah wrapped things up, he caught sight of Ella on the patio and waved. He'd tried to stay away from her after Foster's capture, but he kept being drawn back to her. And Robbie. The boy reminded him of how he'd been growing up. Eager to learn. Curious about everything. Robbie loved Alaska as much as he did. It was one big outdoor park with so much to offer.

"Are you guys ready to leave?" Ella asked as she crossed the yard to them.

"Yes. I can't wait to get my own tent." Robbie grinned from ear to ear, excitement bubbling out of him.

Josiah needed that. To find the joy in life that had been beaten out of him. To truly reconnect with God. "Let's take my truck. Your gear will easily fit in the back."

Rush-hour traffic had subsided, and he drove to the main store in less than fifteen minutes. The moment he entered, an employee approached to help them.

Josiah waved the man away. "Thanks, but I'll take care of this. I know where everything is." He'd been spending more time in the corporate offices and had lost touch with some of the day-to-day activities of the stores. Maybe he needed to become more involved.

"First we need to pick out a tent."

Robbie immediately went to an orange, brown and white dome tent. "I like this one."

Josiah smiled. "That's a good choice. Big enough for up to four people but not too big."

Ella's son beamed. "What's next?"

An hour later, Josiah pushed a cart toward the front while Ella had a second one. He got in line behind a woman with two kids. A large man, similar in build to Foster, came up behind Ella.

With Robbie next to him, Josiah put his hand on his shoulder. The boy had said little about Foster since the day they'd talked in the bathroom, but from the nightmares he'd had at first, Robbie still needed to talk about it. He, of all people, knew that took time. He wanted to be there for the boy when he did.

When Robbie glanced back at Ella, he stiffened.

Josiah squeezed his shoulder gently. "All right?"

"For a second I thought that man was Foster. He isn't." The child took a deep breath. "I'm okay."

"If you ever need to talk, I'm here."

Robbie slanted a look up at Josiah. "Thanks."

"Remember the other day I gave you my cell phone number in case something happens to Sam or you're having a problem with him? Well, you can use it for yourself, too."

The bright light returned to the boy's eyes. He

thrust out his chest and moved up to the clerk to check out.

After the woman rang up the merchandise, he started to pay for the purchases, but Ella quickly moved forward and handed the woman her credit card.

"I wanted to do this for you and Robbie."

"No way. I appreciate the thought, but I'm taking care of it."

"At least let me use my employee discount."

She peered at him for a few seconds, and he wasn't sure if she would even accept that, but then she nodded. He gave the clerk his employee discount information.

When the woman realized who he was, she blushed. "I didn't realize you were Josiah Witherspoon. So sorry, sir." She hurried to finish the transaction.

As they were leaving, Josiah paused and looked at her nametag. "Pam, thank you for doing such a good job."

As he left the store, pushing one of the carts full of items, he said to Ella, "I need to become more involved with my employees. Make sure they feel important. We're growing, and I don't know the new people working for me like I should."

"How many are there?"

"Three hundred and two."

"That's a lot of faces."

"I know their names on paper, but I've only dealt with the employee representatives."

Ella started unloading her cart and putting the supplies in the back of the truck. "You could always do what David does and have a big shindig once a year."

"Yeah, I love that picnic. The softball game is so much fun." Robbie tossed the ground cloth into the pickup's bed.

"It's a good suggestion, and one of the many parks in Anchorage would be a great place to host it."

The idea of having an annual celebration at the end of the summer season felt right. Since returning to Alaska, he'd held himself back from connecting with others, only stepping out of his comfort zone to help with Northern Frontier Search and Rescue, and even then, he often searched with just Buddy.

It was time to reconnect with the world again.

Ella stared out the window of David's plane at the forest-covered island with mountains jutting up in the middle of it. It was green everywhere she looked. Beautiful. Although she hadn't camped since she was a child, she was getting excited about it.

"We're gonna stay here?" Robbie asked Josiah, her son's eyes big as he took in the eastern shore. "Do people live here?"

"Some. Not many. Hunters and visitors come in the summer, though, so we may run into a few people. But essentially, we're bringing in what we need and will take it back out, even our trash."

David landed on the water of the gulf and steered the floatplane to shore. "I'm going to be back here on Sunday evening to take you all home. Six o'clock. Have fun."

"Yippee, we've got two and a half days of camping." Robbie pumped his fist into the air while Alex exited the seaplane, then Josiah.

Her son hopped down, splashing in the few inches of water David landed in. Robbie hurried toward Josiah.

"Are you ready for this?" David asked with a laugh.

"I'm relying on the others to know what to do. Robbie needs this time away, and I'm glad we know people who have camped a lot. See you on Sunday evening, and thanks for dropping us off." Ella climbed out of the airplane as Josiah came back, minus his gear, to get the rest from the back of the plane.

Josiah placed his arms under her and carried her toward shore. "No sense in your boots getting wet. There'll be enough times when we cross a stream."

"Is that why you told me to bring more than three pairs of socks?"

"Smart woman." He set her on the small beach, then returned to the plane to grab the inflatable boat packed in a duffel bag. When Josiah had retrieved all their provisions, he waved to David. "Last chance to go back to civilization." Josiah planted himself next to her and watched as their friend took off.

"Is that what the boat is for? If we have an emergency, we can leave by paddling to the mainland." Ella pointed to the left and in the distance, only miles away, she saw the outline of the Alaskan coast.

"I'm stashing the boat bag in the bushes. Since this isn't Grand Central Station, I don't think a thief will be walking around and stumble upon it, but I like to be prepared for emergencies."

"We could have brought one of David's SAR satellite phones."

Josiah leaned close and placed his forefinger over

his mouth. "Shh. I didn't want Alex getting distracted with business. This is for her as much as Robbie. Besides, if someone goes missing, David would need the few he has for a search and rescue operation." He dragged the duffel bag to the thick brush at the edge of the spruce forest lining the beach. "This will be a perfect place for the boat."

"So no rivers to go down?" Ella asked, anxious but excited about this new experience.

"Nope." He arranged the branches to hide the green bag. "Only a few streams. I have a place in mind to set up camp, and then we can explore from there."

"Mom, are you ready? Alex has been here before, and she's going to be the leader."

"I'll be right behind you." Ella adjusted her backpack, glad the temperature was quickly nearing sixty degrees. Perfect hiking weather.

"And I'll take up the rear," Josiah whispered into her ear.

A shiver streaked down her neck and spine. The idea he was right behind her sent her heart beating faster.

Ella followed her son into the woods off the shore, the light dimming from the dense foliage surrounding her. As she hiked, the scent of the trees and vegetation infused the air, and the sounds of the birds calling echoed through the forest. As she inhaled the fresh smells and drank in her peaceful surroundings, serenity flowed through her. She hadn't felt this in years, not since she was a child. She might not be a good camper, but she was glad she'd come. She needed this.

Two hours later, in an open area at the base of a

mountain, Josiah stopped, sliding his backpack off his shoulders. "This will be home for the next couple of days." He pointed toward the rock face behind him. "On the other side of the ridge is a waterfall that feeds a pond. Farther down the south side is a lighthouse on the cliff."

As her son listened to Josiah talk about the island and what to expect to see, especially the animals, Alex said, "He should be a guide leading groups into the backcountry. I'm surprised he ever left Alaska. It's in his blood."

"It's home. I can understand that, even though I've only been here four years."

"I don't know if I could ever leave here."

"What made Josiah?"

"He wanted to serve his country. Harry was a big influence on him as he grew up, so after he finished college, he enlisted in the military. But the man who came back to Alaska was a changed person," Alex whispered almost to herself, surprise flittering across her expression. She turned, wide-eyed, to Ella. "I shouldn't have said anything. He doesn't talk about his time in the Marines much. All our lives we've been close except for those ten years he was gone. Please don't say anything to him."

"I won't," Ella said. "If he doesn't want to talk about his past, that's his prerogative." But that didn't mean she had to stay around, waiting for something that wasn't going to happen.

Forcing someone to do something would never work in the long run. Keith had used force with her all the time, and finally she'd managed to escape. She knew the situations were different, but after the camping trip, she had to find a way to look at Josiah as only a friend. If not, she'd need to cut her ties completely. She was falling in love with him in spite of trying not to. The very thought sent a bolt of fear through her as all the peace she'd been feeling fled under the memories of her first marriage, based on secrets and lies from the beginning.

"Let's give them some time to bond. Let's put up our tent, then I want to show you a place I loved when I last came."

"I'm glad we decided the guys should share a tent and we girls bunk together. Two tents to carry in are better than three."

"I heard Josiah had to curtail what you were bringing."

As she and Alex worked, Ella said, "I packed my backpack and still had half of the items scattered around me on the floor. Necessary things like a flashlight, insect repellant that I didn't have room for in the bag. I quickly got a lesson on what was essential and what wasn't. I finally convinced him that my moisturizer was important because it was also a sunblock."

"One of the hardest things for me to leave behind was my cell phone. I feel lost without a connection to the outside world. Josiah insisted I not even bring it in the car, so it's sitting on the dresser in my bedroom." Alex chuckled. "I have it bad. But in my defense I run a big business and have a lot of employees."

Ella wished she'd had a sister like Alex, but she'd grown up an only child. She didn't want Robbie growing up like that.

As Alex and she finished erecting the tent, Robbie came over to her. "You did good, Mom. Josiah is gonna let me put up ours and only help if I need it."

Ella ruffled her son's hair. "Ask for help if you need it. That's what you're here for—to learn, so when we go by ourselves we'll know what to do."

He looked at her in all seriousness. "I'm here to have fun. That's what Josiah said."

"Then have fun putting up the tent. Alex and I are going to do some exploring. We'll be back in a little while."

Josiah approached. "Where are you two going?"

Ella nodded her head toward Alex, who was laying the canvas floor down and crawling out of the tent. "She knows. I'm just tagging along."

Alex rose, dusted off her jeans and glanced at her brother. "Overlooking the stream. You know where. Join us when you're through if you all want."

As Robbie went to retrieve the tent. Josiah said in a low voice, "Don't forget to take your gun."

Alex grinned. "Have I ever?"

"Should I bring my revolver, too? It's in my back-pack." Ella glanced at her belongings.

"I thought you were leaving that at your house. Alex and I have our rifles. That should be enough. There haven't been any problems with the bears on this island. The weapons are more a precaution."

"Just so you two know, I'm capable of using a weapon. I learned after I divorced my husband."

With her binoculars hanging around her neck, Alex slung her rifle over her shoulder, plopped her hat on her head and said, "Let's go. Bring your camera in-stead. You should get some great wildlife pictures."

Ella grabbed her camera and water and quickly followed Alex. "We'll see you all in a while."

Forty minutes later, after hiking up a trail that led to an overhang that overlooked a stream, Ella collapsed on a rock perch. "I thought it was a short walk."

"By distance it is. It's the terrain that makes it longer."

"Yeah, climbing up a small mountain for a gal who sits behind a desk most days is a bit of a challenge. How do you keep in shape? You have a desk job, too."

"I work out when I can, and in the winter cross-country skiing keeps me fit. I sometimes ski to work."

"That's something I could do, but not to work. Twice this winter I had to pick up Robbie unexpectedly from school because he was sick."

"You have a terrific kid, Ella. Having him in the house a couple of weeks ago made me realize I'd love to be a mother one day. I suppose I could look at adopting."

"Or marrying again."

Alex stared at the treetops of the forest across the stream. "No, my husband was my high school sweetheart. Since I was a sophomore, I knew I would marry him. I had five fabulous years with Cade. I can't see myself finding anyone to fill his shoes in my life."

"You never know."

Alex slanted a look at Ella. "How about you? You're a great mother to Robbie. Don't you want more children?"

"I'd love to, but for different reasons I don't see myself marrying again, either."

Alex opened her mouth, but instead of saying anything snapped it closed.

A noise behind Ella drew her around. Robbie appeared on the trail with Josiah right behind him. "What took you all so long?"

"We got some wood for a fire after setting up our tent. So now all you two have to do is fix dinner. Both of us—" Josiah pointed at Robbie then himself "—are hungry. We worked up an appetite."

"First, I'm going to take some photos." Ella lifted her camera to her face. "I'll cook if you agree to clean up."

A black-tailed deer came down to the water about ten yards upstream. She took several pictures as two more joined the first one.

She gestured toward the animals when a fawn moved out of the foliage. "Robbie, a baby deer. Do you see it?"

Robbie sat near her. "It's so cute. I hope no bears are around."

"So do I." Josiah stood behind her son.

Alex passed the binoculars to Robbie. "Take a look through these. You can see the black tails better and the spots on the fawn."

Ella rose to move closer to the ledge. As long as she wasn't at the very edge, she was all right with the height. She wanted to see if anything was on this side of the water. Suddenly all the deer looked up, then raced back into the forest. *What scared them? A bear?* She scanned up and down the stream. The sunlight glinted off something for a second, then disappeared.

"Can I have the binoculars, Robbie, for a minute?"

Her son held them up for her. She took them, then swung around to locate the dense vegetation across the water downstream where she thought she'd seen something—some*one*. It couldn't have been a bear. Then, in the midst of the thick undergrowth, she spied an individual, almost totally camouflaged, with binoculars directed toward them.

"We have company."

TWELVE

When Ella moved nearer to the ledge, keeping the binoculars fixed on the same spot, Josiah closed the space between them. "Found something interesting?"

She turned her head toward him, sliding a glance toward Robbie, then passing the binoculars to Josiah. "I saw someone in that brush down there." She pointed downstream about fifty feet.

He followed the direction she indicated, but he didn't see anyone. "Whoever it was is gone now. Although not many people live on this island, it does get some campers, hunters and hikers. We'll probably run into some while hiking tomorrow. Could be someone looking for deer. It's hunting season."

Suddenly the noise of a gunshot split the air. Ella jerked back, brushing up against Josiah, her hand splaying across her chest.

Josiah clasped her upper arms. "You okay?"

"That stopped my heart. I hope the guy missed, if he's a hunter."

"Mom, Alex and I are heading to camp, but you should stay and take a few more pictures. Maybe you'll get one of a bear."

Ella's eyes narrowed. "I get the feeling those two are conspiring."

Josiah laughed. "When I moved over here to see what you were looking at, they kept exchanging glances, so I'd say you're right."

Another shot rang out. Ella tensed. "You'd think I'd be used to hearing gunfire since I practice at the shooting range. But coming out of the blue like that..."

He leaned close to her ear and lowered his voice. "We'll hear that occasionally this weekend. You'll learn to tune it out."

"Never. Even on the shooting range, I'm aware of every shot fired. When my ex took me there, Keith liked to demonstrate his 'gift,' as he put it. But what it was really was another intimidation technique."

Josiah squeezed her arm gently. "Don't think about him. He's not here, so don't let him ruin your vacation."

She looked back at him. "I know, but no matter how much I try to put him out of my mind, at odd moments he intrudes."

"Don't let him win. You lived in fear for four years. You don't have to now."

She rotated toward him. "How about you? Something has happened to you. By all accounts, I've heard you aren't the same person you were when you went into the Marines. I know you served several tours of duty in the war zone. I also know you don't like to talk about it. I was like that, too. Confiding in you was one of the best things I've ever done. Of course, I can't go around telling the world, since I'm in hiding, but having one person know is enough. I felt a burden lifted from my shoulders. Let me help you, Josiah. And if not me, at least talk to Alex."

"She knows some of it." He stepped away.

"But not all?"

He pursed his lips and averted his gaze. "I can't. I…" He felt as though he was on the side of a cliff, ready to rappel down the rock face, and yet he couldn't make that first move and step off. He wanted to, but something held him back. The memories were buried deep, where he wanted to keep them, and yet…

She started for the path down the mountain.

"Ella."

She turned to him, expectation on her face.

"Wait up. I'll hike down with you."

A mask fell over her features, but not before he saw the hurt in her gaze. She'd given him a part of herself when she'd told him about her husband, but the words inside him were dammed up behind a protective wall.

"That's okay. I'd rather be alone." An impregnable expression met his appraisal. "We're friends, but that's all. I know that, but as a friend, I wanted to help. Now I know my boundaries."

Although her look didn't reveal much, her voice cracked on the last sentence. She swung around and marched down the trail. He'd give her a minute and follow her, staying back a hundred yards. But he wanted to keep an eye on her. He had a rifle; she didn't.

As she descended the mountain, she called over her shoulder, "What part of *alone* do you not understand? I figured you knew that definition well."

He sucked in a breath and slowed his pace, catching sight of her every minute or so on the winding path.

Lord, why can't I talk about it?

As he came into camp, he knew the answer. If he acknowledged out loud the brutality he'd endured, it would be real. It was bad enough that the memories dwelled in his mind. All he wanted to do was swipe them clean from his thoughts. Hatred toward his captors jammed his throat, and when his sister asked him a question about dinner, he couldn't answer.

A fist rose above Ella's head and came crashing down on her, pounding her over and over while Josiah watched, his arms held behind him by an unseen force. He screamed out to her to hold on and struggled with his invisible bonds.

Ella tried to bolt up, but something trapped her to the ground. She clawed at it. Her eyes flew open, a faint light streaming through the tent flaps, as she wrestled with her sleeping bag. Her breath came out in short pants, her chest rising and falling rapidly. Slowly she orientated herself to her surroundings.

Alex still slept soundly two feet away from her. She was camping with Robbie. Josiah. The thought of him broke her heart. He was unreachable. She couldn't fall in love with a man who kept his life hidden from her. She'd shared her dark past and felt better that she finally had because she'd trusted Josiah with her secret.

But he didn't trust her.

She slid her eyes closed for a long moment, trying to compose herself before getting up. After her dream, she wasn't going back to sleep even if the time was only—she glanced at her watch—5:15 a.m. At least it was daylight. She could check the food supplies and plan what she would make for breakfast. Put on a pot of coffee. She needed it to stay awake.

She walked to the edge of the campsite and yanked on the rope that held their food in a tarp off the ground. It wasn't nearly as heavy as she thought it would be. She brought it to the ground and moved to pick the items she would need. When she flipped the canvas top away, she gasped. All she found were rocks.

All the food was gone.

For a long moment, she knelt on the tarp, stunned.

She heard a movement behind her. She swiveled around, wishing she had her gun with her.

Yawning, Josiah approached. "What's wrong?"

"Our food has been stolen, and not by bears." She leaned to the side so he could see.

His eyes grew huge, and a thunderous expression chased all sleepiness from his face. "Is this how you found it? On the ground?"

She pushed the cover totally off the rocks. "No, it was hanging in the air with these in it. Someone deliberately stole our food and left us rocks."

"This has got to be a joke. Alex has played some on me in the past."

"Like this?"

"Well, not exactly." He strode to her tent and stuck his head inside.

Not a minute later, Alex emerged and charged over to the tarp to inspect what happened. "I'd never do this. I love my food more than you do."

"I wish Buddy was here. I'd like to track down who did this." His scowl evened out a little, and he pulled the tarp off the ground. "I might be able to follow the tracks." He looked at the forest around them and headed back to his tent.

When he came out with a flashlight, probably to use in the dimly lit forest, Robbie was right behind him, rubbing his eyes. Josiah grabbed his rifle and held it in one hand as if he were ready to use it at a second's notice.

"I'll be back."

"Can I come with you?" Robbie asked, starting to follow Josiah.

He turned to her son, clasping his shoulder. "You need to stay here. Help your mom and Alex. I'll be back in a little while. Okay?"

Robbie nodded.

As he left, Alex put one hand on her waist. "We need to start looking for something to eat. I saw some berries not far up the trail. Let's start there, then we can pull out our poles and try to catch some fish when Josiah comes back."

"That'll be a healthy breakfast."

"But, Mom, I hate fish."

Josiah found boot prints that led to the stream, but as he stood on the edge of the flowing water, he was afraid the trail had ended. In many places, the stream wasn't deeper than his thighs, so someone could go ashore in countless places. The freezing water numbed his legs as he started downstream first, not even sure if the thief had crossed to the other side or only used the water as a means to throw him off his trail. Finally, an hour later, he made his way back to the camp, not wanting to be gone any longer.

Ella saw him first and hurried over. "Did you find anything?"

"He used the stream to cover his tracks. I didn't see where he came out, but there were places he could have found stones. I saw footprints but not like the ones I found going away from our camp. To be honest, the guy could have taken his boots off. I figure we should forget about him and enjoy ourselves. He didn't get our bottled water at least."

"We found some berries, and Alex is ready to go fishing. Robbie is all excited. He feels as if he's living off the land like a survivalist."

"Leave it to a child to turn our thinking around. It's a challenge, but one we can deal with. We had a big dinner last night. We have clean water and a stream with fish in it. And to top it off, we can have dessert—berries."

"And we have each other—*friends* enjoying a weekend away from the rat race."

The emphasis on *friends* didn't miss the mark with Josiah. After last night at the bluff, he knew he would always remain broken, and there was no way he would ever enter into a relationship with a woman, especially one with a child, when part of him couldn't shake the hate that kept him locked in a prison of his own making. He wanted to see all of his captors rot in a cell until they breathed their last breath. That realization stunned him. He hadn't known how deep his anger went until now.

"Josiah, are you all right?" Ella touched his arm.

The feel of her fingers on his skin shocked him from his thoughts. He blinked, trying to tamp down the emotions reeling through him. He'd never have a full life without finding a way to forgive his captors. He didn't know what to say to Ella.

She looked long and hard at him, then went to Alex and Robbie to help them with the fishing equipment.

For a moment he watched them, unable to move, to think beyond what he'd discovered about himself. Had Ella forgiven her ex-husband? Or was she stuck in limbo like him? Unable to move forward with his life?

"Josiah, we're ready," Robbie called out.

"I'm coming," he finally said, shutting his past back into the dark recesses of his mind. He was going to have fun right now, and examine his life later when he was back in Anchorage. "I'm hungry. Let's go get some breakfast."

Later, Ella stuck the trash in a plastic bag to take with them when they left the island. "Robbie, did you get enough food?"

Her son swiped the back of his hand across his mouth. "I'm stuffed. Josiah, the salmon was great."

"This from a boy who less than twenty-four hours ago declared he hated fish. Obviously when you're starving, you'll eat anything." Ella finished cleaning up their used paper products. "Who wants to walk with me to the stream to wash our pan out?"

"I will," Josiah said before anyone else. "Alex and Robbie can get more firewood."

"I think we got the raw end of this deal." Alex stood. "C'mon, Robbie, let's get it so we can sit around relaxing. I promised to tell you about my first search and rescue with Sadie."

Ella had purposefully stayed away from Josiah all day while they'd fished, hiked and gathered a few edible items to complement the salmon. Now she was stuck walking with him. She started toward the stream. He snatched his rifle and hurried after her.

"Wait up. I'm supposed to be your guard."

"In case the thief comes back to steal our skillet?"

"He could. Or a bear could be fishing for salmon. A better place for fishing is farther upstream, but you never know."

"Sheesh, thanks. Now I'm going to be on pins and needles the whole time."

"Right now, the bears are focused on eating all the salmon they can before winter."

Ella kept walking, concentrating on each step she took rather than the man to the left and slightly behind her. The sound of the water rushing over the rocks lured her closer and closer to the stream. She'd wash the pan and quickly return to camp.

If there had been a way to leave the island, she would have. But she had less than a day before David picked them up. She'd have to deal with being in close confines with Josiah until then, but once she returned to Anchorage, she would keep her distance. She realized she was falling in love with Josiah, but this morning, when she'd tried once more to reach out to him, he'd rejected her. She'd seen that look of pain and vulnerability on his face right before going fishing. But all she'd met was a wall of silence.

"Ella, could you slow down? We don't have to jog to the stream." Josiah's request cut through her thoughts.

"Why? I want to wash this—" she waved the skillet "—and get back to camp. It's been a long day, and I'm ready to sleep."

"It's not even eight o'clock and still bright outside."

She came to an abrupt halt and swirled around. "What do you want from me? You've been sending me mixed messages all day. I can't keep doing this." The words exploded from her as if she'd released the built-up pressure in a carbonated drink.

"To talk."

"Now?" Her gaze drilled into him. She tried desperately to read in his expression what was behind that request. But he was too good at hiding his emotions.

"Yes. I've angered you, and I think we should talk about it."

"Just go back to camp. Leave me alone."

She charged toward the stream at a fast clip. She wasn't going to argue with him. At the creek, she knelt by the edge, dipped her skillet in the water and swished it around, letting the rapid current wash the bits of food away.

Josiah squatted next to her and covered his hand over hers, grasping the pan. He took it and placed it on the ground, then drew her around. "Please hear me out."

The soft plea in his eyes was her undoing. She nodded.

He rose and tugged her away from the rushing stream to a pile of smooth stones. Taking a seat on one, he patted the rock next to him. When she sat, he clasped her hand and turned toward her. Her heartbeat sped like the flowing water.

He inhaled a deep breath and let it out slowly. "I'm not even sure where to begin. I've only shared part of what I'm going to tell you with two people—my sister and the counselor I saw for a year. It isn't common knowledge that I was a prisoner of war for months because my mission was a secret one behind enemy lines. I can't talk about it even now."

"You were a POW?" She'd known he must have gone through some horrific situations while in the Marines, but not that.

"Yes. I was captured and beaten for the details of my mission. When I finally broke, I was thrown into a cell only three feet by three feet. I hated myself for breaking down and tried to console myself with the fact that, by that time, the information I'd given them didn't mean anything. All I wanted at first was for them to kill me. End my pain."

Ella had once thought that herself, after her husband had pushed her down the stairs and she'd broken both arms. Then she'd remembered Robbie, who'd only been three at that time, and knew she had to protect him. She'd begun fighting back then and making secret plans to get away. She cupped her other hand on top of their clasped ones.

"I can tell you every gory detail of captivity if you really want to know."

Tears filling her eyes, she shook her head. "No, there's no need. The fact that you would is all I care about. My relationship with Keith was full of secrets and lies. I care so much for you, Josiah. I didn't want anything to stand between us, or I would never have told you about my ex-husband."

He captured her chin and caressed the tears away with his thumb. "After a while I turned to the Lord, begging Him to end my suffering. He didn't. Instead, slowly I felt my fighting spirit return. I thought of

Alex. I thought of my fiancée, Lori, who I was going to marry when I returned from the mission. Suddenly what they did to me didn't mean anything anymore. I had a goal—to escape. To return home. And the Lord would help me."

Like I did. The power of God overwhelmed her. She couldn't stop the flow of tears running down her face, splashing onto their entwined fingers.

"The Lord was with me in that cell. Lately I've forgotten that. I was letting the traumatic past haunt me, letting it drive a wedge between me and God. But not anymore. I know what I have to do. I have to forgive my captors."

She wanted to hold him, but she was afraid that would be a distraction. His greatest need at the moment was to talk about his past. "How did you escape?"

"I could tell something was going on in the camp. A flurry of activity. Many days went by when I never saw my jailer. On the day I made my escape, a young boy brought me water and food." He stared off into space as though he was seeing it all again in his mind.

She stroked her thumb over the curve of his hand. "What happened next?"

His gaze returned to hers, awe in the depths of his crystal-blue eyes. "There was a commotion outside the cave. The boy hurriedly left, and I guess he didn't lock the door correctly. After I ate, I went to the door to see if I could hear anything. That's when I discovered it was unlocked. Without a second thought, I left my prison and managed to sneak away."

"How long did it take before you made it to safety?"

"Just hours. The commotion was a force of our

men drawing near their cave hideout. The terrorists were trying to get away."

"Did they?"

"Some did. Others were killed or captured. At least that's what I heard. Our troops called for help when they found me at the bottom of the mountain. A helicopter took me back to the base. Then my journey to healing began."

"And look where you are now. Helping others. Me." She tugged him toward her and wrapped her arms around him. "I'm so sorry for what happened to you. I wish I could erase that part of your past."

He pulled slightly away and framed her face. "And I wish I could erase parts of yours. Have you been able to forgive Keith? Because I don't know how to take that step. If I don't forgive my captors, I'll never be whole again."

She closed her eyes, wishing she could help him. "I haven't forgiven Keith yet. I've prayed to God to help me, but so far I'm still as angry as I was after I managed to get away from him."

"Do you think we have a chance to be more than friends?" The feel of his thumb as it whispered across her cheek tempted her. But she couldn't. "I don't know. I'm afraid our pasts will always be there as a barrier to the true, loving relationship we deserve. I don't know if I can ever let go of the fear and mistrust I have because of Keith."

His hands slipped away from her face. He clenched them, and the strong, tense set to his jawline shouted he felt that way about his situation, too. "The reason I have Buddy is because he was—really still is—a service dog for a person with post-traumatic stress disorder. I still occasionally have nightmares and panic attacks. Not often, but enough to remind me I'm still far from healed. When I came home, I desperately wanted what happened to me to go away as if it had never occurred. When I got out of the hospital, I went to see Lori. I didn't want anyone to tell her I was home until I could see her myself. I didn't want her to see me in the hospital."

"When you love someone, that shouldn't matter."

He looked into her eyes, his stiff posture relaxing slightly, but tension still poured off him. "I know. In the end it didn't really matter. She'd already moved on and was in love with another man. Thoughts of a life with her were one of the ways I kept myself going while a prisoner, but I realize I've forgiven Lori. I wasn't in any shape to be in a relationship when I returned to the States anyway."

Her throat swelled with emotions. Ella fought the tears rising inside. She couldn't stop them.

He took her into his embrace and pressed her against his chest. The pounding of his heart beneath her ear finally calmed the tears to a whimper. "We are quite a pair," she murmured. "What are we going to do?"

"Maybe when we get back to Anchorage, we should spend some time apart. We both need to figure out what we really want for ourselves and find a way to make it happen."

She leaned away and stared into his eyes, realizing these past weeks she had been fighting the feelings that had developed in spite of her trying to avoid an emotional involvement. In spite of her fear, she'd make the same mistake as she had with Keith. "I love you, Josiah, but I'm not sure that's enough. I can't make a mistake about this because it doesn't just affect me. I have Robbie to consider, too."

Josiah bent forward and kissed her lightly, but before he could deepen it, he put some space between them. "I agree. I never want him to be hurt."

"Then what do we tell him when you suddenly stop coming around?"

"I'll think of something, but for the time being let's just enjoy each other's company for the rest of this trip. Going camping was important to Robbie."

"I can do that." On overload with all that had transpired, Ella rose from the rock. "Are you ready to go back? They're probably wondering what's keeping us."

"Yes." He stood, taking her hand.

When she glanced upstream, she gasped and froze. Three brown bears were in the water catching salmon. "Have they been there the whole time?"

"Yes, but I was keeping an eye on them."

She'd been so focused on Josiah she hadn't even been aware of the huge animals only a football field away. Josiah did that to her. And yet, he also protected her.

As Ella strolled back to camp, she kept glancing over her shoulder. Although she'd lived here four years, it wasn't a common occurrence for her to see three brown bears at one time. But she saw no sign of them being bothered by her and Josiah. As she neared their campsite, she began to relax.

"What are we going to do tomorrow?" she asked, finally breaking the silence between them.

"There's a place we can sit on the shore and watch

for whales. I can't guarantee we'll see them, but we can try. I think Robbie will get a big kick out of that."

"He certainly was excited about seeing the bald eagle in the tree today."

"That excited me. A majestic bird. Being around Robbie has renewed the awe I used to have while growing up here. You have a special son."

Suddenly a gunshot reverberated through the woods. Coming to a sudden stop, Ella tensed. "That was close."

Another blast rang out.

"It's coming from the direction of our campsite," Josiah said, grasping his rifle with both of his hands as he set out in a jog.

THIRTEEN

The pounding of Ella's footsteps matched his as Josiah raced toward the camp. As he came closer, he slowed, the beating of his heart thundering in his ears.

On the outskirts, he crept forward, Ella mirroring him. Alex stood with Robbie in front of a rocky facade, a piece of paper stuck on a small tree limb. She was demonstrating how to handle a rifle. A look of deep concentration was on the boy's face.

Ella moved around him, headed toward the pair across the campsite and said with a laugh, "You should warn me before you start target practice."

Robbie whirled toward her. "Alex was showing me how good she is. I drew a bull's-eye on the paper. She hit it twice. I want to learn. Can I, Mom?"

Alex faced Ella and Josiah. "We got bored waiting for you two to come back. Robbie wanted to know about my gun. I was pointing out how it worked and why we carry it when we go into the backcountry."

Ella turned to Robbie, a solemn expression on her face. "When you're older. Until then, you aren't to handle one. I imagine from Alex's demonstration you see how dangerous a weapon can be in the wrong hands or with someone who doesn't know what he's doing. Okay?"

With an equally somber expression, Robbie nodded.

"If we had our food, right about now, we'd be roasting marshmallows and making s'mores," Josiah said to lighten the moment of seriousness. "But we have some berries left instead. Anybody up for finishing them off with me?"

Robbie giggled. "What about breakfast tomorrow morning?"

"We'll need much more than berries tomorrow." Josiah drew the boy toward the fire ring. "We have over an hour's hike to a place I want to show you. We'll need to leave early, so I'm going to get up at the crack of dawn and go fishing. Want to come with me?"

"If you're gonna tell me where we're going to hike."

"Hopefully to see whales."

As Robbie sat near the dying fire, his eyes grew huge. "Really?"

"Maybe seals, some more eagles, too."

Robbie clapped. "Yes!"

Ella joined Josiah and Robbie, taking a seat next to her son. "I gather you're going fishing, then."

Robbie twisted toward her with his solemn expression on his face. "If we're gonna have breakfast, I have to. I'm the one who caught the most fish today."

"I think you threw down the gauntlet, Robbie." Ella's eyes twinkled.

"Gauntlet? What's that?" her son asked.

"A glove. In olden times when someone did that, it

meant they were challenging another person to something." Ella glanced toward Josiah.

He smiled. "And I take up that challenge. I'm going to catch more fish than you by seven o'clock. Deal?" Josiah held out his hand.

Her son shook it. "Deal."

"While you two battle it out at the stream, Alex and I will sleep in and have a blazing fire going by the time you come back in anticipation of all the fish you're going to catch. Now, I wonder who can top me in telling the tallest tale."

Josiah lounged back on his elbows as first his sister and then Robbie took up the dare. Around the fire, with the sun going down, the leaves rustling in the cool breeze and the sound of insects and birds filling the air, he thought about what he had told Ella at the stream. As he'd gone through the details of his ordeal, he'd always thought it would send him into a panic attack. It had when he'd first talked with his counselor. It had when he'd shared some of it with Alex. Would his nightmare return tonight with Buddy at home?

Josiah caught Ella staring at him, her warm brown eyes probing, as though trying to reach into his mind. He averted his gaze. He didn't want to let her go, but he didn't think he was good for her.

The next morning Ella woke up, snuggled comfortably in her sleeping bag. She'd gotten a good night's rest and was ready for the day of hiking before David came at six to pick them up. This weekend had been a revelation—from Josiah, but also inside her. Somewhere deep within her, she needed to find a way to let go of her anger toward Keith and move on completely.

Josiah was right. She could never truly embrace the rest of her life if she didn't.

Sitting up, Ella stretched the kinks out of her body, which wasn't used to sleeping on the hard ground. Even as she crawled from the tent, she continued to work out the stiffness from her muscles. She spied Alex sitting on the ground, her eyes closed, her body relaxed. She'd learned when living at the estate that Alex always meditated first thing in the morning if possible. It was her special time with God. Ella liked that idea, but she found the end of the day worked best for her.

When Ella stood, Alex opened her eyes. Ella quickly said, "I'm gathering the firewood we need. Go back to what you're doing."

Ella hurried into the wooded area near the campsite as Alex slid her eyelids closed again. She'd slept so well she hadn't heard Josiah or Robbie leaving at sunrise to fish. Glancing at her watch, she knew the guys would be back in about twenty minutes, ready to cook the fish. Bending over, she began picking up stray tree limbs until her arms were loaded with firewood.

She heard an owl in an upper branch of one of the trees and stopped, trying to determine where he was perched. Another hoot echoed through the woods. Suddenly she thought about what had started all of this—falling in love with a man who wasn't ready for a relationship. It had been weeks ago when Robbie and his friends went in search of an owl. Something good had come out of the incident with Foster. Maybe sometime later, Josiah and she would have a chance.

I hope so.

let go of the hold Keith had
...ould do that because she and
...re. She leaned over to grab one
...od before heading back to camp. She
...nd swung around to retrace her steps
...aw him.

...collected firewood tumbled to the ground
...t her feet.

Keith.

With a rifle pointed at her.

"I won. I won." Robbie danced around in circles at the stream.

Josiah laughed at the glee on the boy's face. "You're a natural outdoorsman. The skills will come as you get older. That doesn't have anything to do with being a natural."

Robbie puffed out his chest. "Can I learn how to cook these salmon you filleted?"

"Sure. Let's go." Josiah washed his hands in the stream, grabbed the fish he'd prepared and headed toward the campsite.

"Thanks, Josiah, for showing me all these things this weekend. Mom isn't too big on camping, but when I get older, I'll be able to go with friends."

"Until then, you can go with me again, if you like," Josiah said, before he realized Ella probably wouldn't want that. Yesterday evening, they had agreed to put some distance between them.

"I'd love that."

They walked through the woods in silence for a while, then Robbie asked, "Do you like my mom?"

Josiah could answer many questions about Alaska,

dogs and camping, but that question left him spe
less. He couldn't lie to the boy, but he didn't war
give him false hope concerning him and Ella. "I thi
your mom is very special," he finally said, prayin
that would satisfy Robbie.

"Would you ever consider being my dad?"

Stunned, Josiah came to a halt. He opened his
mouth to say something, but couldn't think of a reply.

The child stopped, too. "I know you two haven't
dated long—"

"We haven't really dated at all."

"Well, you have my permission to date my mom."
Robbie started again for the campsite.

It took a moment for Josiah to gather his wits.
What was he going to say to Ella about this? Then the
thought of being the child's father began to worm its
way into his mind. He finally trailed a few feet behind
the boy, thinking of the prospect of having a child—
children. Yesterday that thought would have scared
him, but now it didn't sound quite as far-fetched.

When they entered the camp, Alex had her gun in
hand and was starting for the forest on the left.

"Where are you going?"

"Ella has been gone too long. She left to collect the
firewood we needed. That was over half an hour ago."

Josiah walked to her and gave her the fillets. "Get
these ready. I'll track her and bring her back."

As he headed into the trees, he stamped down the
gut feeling something had happened. She might have
gotten turned around in the woods, especially if she'd
wandered too far away.

Ella is all right.

He kept repeating that as he followed her tracks.

* * *

Shocked and frozen, Ella stared into the diamond-hard eyes of her ex-husband, boring into hers with such hatred. No words came to mind. Her heartbeat began to hammer against her rib cage at such a rapid pace she thought it would burst from her chest.

"I've been searching for you for four years." His gaze raked down her length. "Finally I get to pay you back for turning me in."

How had he found her? Fear choked her throat, making it impossible to say anything. All her past nightmares came crashing down on her.

"I'm going to kill you slowly, then take *my son* and raise him to be a man."

Robbie. No, he can't. She tamped down the terror threatening to make her useless. Her son's life was at stake. *Lord, I can't do this without You.*

"What? You have nothing to say to your husband?"

"No." It wouldn't do any good.

He tossed her a set of handcuffs. "Put these on. And make it fast."

They fell at her feet. She glared at him.

"If you don't cooperate with me, I'll make Robbie's life worse than you could ever imagine."

Begrudgingly she bent over and snatched the handcuffs, then snapped them on.

"That's a good little wife. No piece of paper will change that fact." Keith slung the rifle over his shoulder and took out a handgun. "Let's go. I have a nice secluded spot for a special celebration between us."

She shuddered at the sneer in his voice, the evil on his face. How had she ever thought she was in love with this man? Because he had been a master at putting up just the right facade for people—at least for a short time. Then his true nature always came out.

He approached her, gripped her arm and dragged her in front of him. He leaned close to her ear and whispered, "I've been thinking for years about what I would do with you when I finally found you. When you were splashed across the news, you made it so easy for me. You might look different, but Robbie looks just like me." He yanked her long hair tied in a ponytail. "I like this blond color much better than that mousy brown you had. Let's go."

The glee in his voice left her stone-cold. He had to shove her to get her to move. He rammed the barrel into her back and kept prodding her forward through the undergrowth until he came to an animal trail. She knew that Josiah could track, but she wanted to make it as easy as possible. The only thing she had access to was a beaded bracelet Robbie had made her at camp.

As she trudged before Keith, she managed to slip the piece of jewelry off her wrist. She pulled it apart until she held a handful of small beads. Were they large enough for Josiah to see?

Following the set of tracks from the area Alex had indicated, Josiah reached a small clearing and homed in on some scattered branches lying on the ground near a set of her footprints. What had happened here? Why had she dropped the firewood? Had an animal scared her?

He studied the surroundings, taking in the boot prints—similar to the ones he'd tracked after their food had been taken. The tracks stopped right in front of hers. Then they both moved off to the northeast.

His gut twisted and knotted. Ella had been taken. It didn't matter why. He just had to get her back and protect the others. She wouldn't have gone off willingly without letting Alex know.

He raced to the campsite and motioned for Alex to come to him. When she did, he lowered his voice, keeping an eye on Robbie so he wouldn't hear, and said, "Someone took Ella. A large man, by the size of the boot print. I think it's the same man who stole our food. Leave everything, take Robbie and use the inflatable boat to get help on the mainland. The man is taking her northeast."

When she nodded, Josiah snatched up his backpack with binoculars, rope and a flashlight, waved to Robbie, then whirled around and hurried after Ella and her kidnapper. When he reached the small clearing, he began the slow tracking process until he found a yellow bead in the dirt. About twenty yards away, he saw another one—blue.

Ella's legs protested with each step she took. Sweat rolled down her face. Her eyes stung from the saltiness. The constant poking of the gun into her back had become an irritant that made her want to scream out in frustration and fear.

Ahead, a rocky path started to slant upward. She craned her neck at the direction Keith was taking her. She didn't know if she had the energy to go twenty feet up the slope, let alone climb a mountain. But the worst part was how scared she was of heights.

Lord, what do I do?

She slowed her pace at the bottom of the incline. Keith plowed into her.

She fell forward, her knees taking the brunt of the fall onto the stones. Pain shot up her body, and she bit her lower lip to keep from crying out.

"If I have to, I'll drag you up there. Get up. Now."

She placed her fists, one that still clenched the few remaining beads, on the hard surface and pushed herself to her shaky legs. God was with her. She could do this.

"This is for every day I've feared for my life. For my lousy life in the witness security program trying to live on a measly amount of money. But I'm taking my life back. I'm gonna take care of you. Then I'm getting Robbie and leaving the country."

Taunting words filled her mind, but she gritted her teeth to keep them to herself. He'd never be free of the organization he'd worked for because he'd betrayed them. She could only imagine the horrors of what they'd do to a traitor. Even halfway around the world. Somehow she had to find a way to prevent him from getting her son. She wouldn't let Robbie live a life on the run from men bent on murdering Keith.

He shoved her forward, but she managed to keep her balance and tramped up the rocks.

Please, Lord, protect Robbie from Keith. Get him to safety.

She prayed with each step she took up the mountain, her body shaking. She kept her gaze focused on the ground in front of her, not on how far she had come up the incline. She dropped the few beads she had left at the halfway mark of the sixty-degree slope. Part of their ascent was hidden by trees, and she knew they were on the other side of the range from where they had camped.

I'm in Your hands, Lord.

About a hundred yards from the top, Keith propelled her around a large boulder and into a cave in the stone facade. Dark and musky with only one way out, and Keith blocked it, towering over her with a fierce countenance.

His eyes became black pinpoints. "Now we're far enough away from anybody else that even if you screamed no one would hear." He waved his revolver at her. "I have a little place set up just for you. Get up and get moving." Keith gestured toward the black hole that led deeper into the cave.

The last bead Josiah found was a fourth of the way up the side of a mountain. But nothing since. Had he missed the direction Ella and her kidnapper had gone? On a small ledge, he used the binoculars and scanned above him then to the left and right before he surveyed the area below him. Either Ella and her kidnapper had already made it to the top, or they were hiding somewhere on this face of the mountain.

Sweat drenched him. At the moment the only choice he had was to continue straight up and pray the Lord showed him where Ella was. He hoped Alex had gotten Robbie off the island by now. At least Ella's son would be safe.

Since he didn't want to miss Ella and the man who'd taken her, he stopped periodically and panned his surroundings. For the third time he came up empty-handed, and frustration ate at him.

On the fourth survey from the small outcropping where he stood, he sidled carefully to the right, wanting to check out a boulder on a ledge a hundred feet away. Was that an opening? Creeping as far as he could, he held on to a small bush growing out of the side of the mountain to lean as far away from the rock wall as he could.

The second he figured out that the hole in the stone wasn't just a crevice but a cave, the brush pulled away from the rocks. He teetered on the edge, flapping his arms to get his balance.

Deeper in the cave, Ella spied a faint glow up ahead of her; the only light guiding her way was the one Keith wore strapped to his head.

"We aren't far from the cavern I've prepared for us."

They turned a corner, and the faint glow was gone. She couldn't hold her arms out to feel the side of the cave as he did. She took another cautious step, and her foot twisted as it came down between two rocks.

She cried out as she went down, her left arm colliding with a jutting piece of the wall. She fought the tears that welled into her eyes, making what little she could see blurry, and she averted her head before he saw. He'd loved to see her cry and beg. She wouldn't give him the satisfaction.

"Get up." Keith kicked her leg, now pinned between two stones.

Rising anger vied with her fear as she finally yanked her foot free.

"Now."

"I am! If you'd give me a light, I could see where I'm going" were the first words she spoke since he'd asked her if she had anything to say to him.

"Ah, she finally speaks." Mockery laced each of his words.

She struggled to stand, keeping her back to him while she blinked the last of her tears. Her fury was taking over. She wouldn't give up the fight until she drew her last breath.

"As usual, you think you're a big man because you *think* you can cow a woman a foot shorter than you."

He snorted. "I haven't even begun toying with you. To even the playing field a little, I'll give you a head start. I'll count to one hundred while you try to get away from me. I suppose it's possible you could find a hiding place. Who knows? But the only way you can escape is into the mountain."

She finally glanced over her shoulder. The bright light nearly blinded her. The only thing she could see was him holding the gun aimed at her.

"One, two, three. You better get going."

She started forward.

"Four, five, six."

She brought her left arm across her chest so she could run her hands along the side of the wet, cold cave. She tried to block his counting from her mind.

But she couldn't.

"Twenty, twenty-one, twenty-two."

Using the wall as a guide wasn't working well. She gave it up and lifted her arms out in front, then increased her pace. The cave curved to the right, and the glare of his headlamp no longer lit her way, even vaguely. Darkness shrouded her, but she kept going. She needed to find somewhere to hide.

"One hundred. Here I come."

FOURTEEN

Josiah lost his balance and slipped from the ledge. He began to fall down the slope, his arms flailing for a handhold. A stone jutting out from the outcropping grazed his fingers, and he grasped it, stopping his descent down the side of the mountain. He swung his other hand around the rock while his legs dangled in the air. Willing all his strength into his arms, he slowly pulled himself back up to the shelf, his muscles twitching with the strain.

He lay on the rough surface and dragged oxygen into his lungs. He couldn't stay here. He needed to get to that cave and see if Ella was in there. Otherwise she and her kidnapper were already on the ridge, and it would take him a while to pick up their trail. Cautiously he made his way to the right and up.

When he reached the cave's entrance, he checked the ground for any sign Ella was in there. In the dirt just inside the opening, he glimpsed footprints like the ones he'd been tracking. He took a step toward them and halted. Sweat popped out on his forehead. His heartbeat thumped against his chest, and his pulse raced.

Suddenly he was thrust back into the past when he was kept prisoner in a cage in a cave. His legs refused to move forward into the waiting darkness, as though he'd been flash frozen.

Ella groped around another turn, moving away from the glow she'd spied earlier. She wouldn't put it past Keith to have set it up as a lure, knowing he was going to do something like this. The longer she kept Keith away from Robbie, the better the chance her son would get away. Alex and Josiah would know something was wrong by now and go for help.

You're not alone in this. She felt those words deep in her heart. This wasn't the same as before with Keith when she'd become so cut off from friends and family. When Keith found her, he would discover she wasn't the same docile woman he'd terrorized. If she didn't leave this cave, neither would he.

She glanced back and noticed a light coming closer to the turnoff she'd taken. Twisting forward again, she picked up speed, going several yards when her left foot slammed against a rock. Even in her boots, pain zipped up her leg. She stumbled and went down, using her arms to break her fall. At the same time the collision with the wall knocked the breath from her. She labored to sit up and tried to stand. She crumpled to the rock surface, back against the side of the tunnel.

Before trying to rise again, she patted the area around her. She had to hide. Watching the light growing brighter as Keith stalked her, she hoisted herself to her knees and checked the evenness of the floor in front of her. She encountered another rocky obstacle. She crawled forward to see if there were more.

For the next twenty feet she painstakingly made her way from one stone obstruction to another. The path ahead grew narrower.

Until she came to a drop-off. Trapped.

Josiah lifted his foot and moved forward into the cave's entrance. His body shook. His past captors were not going to control him. The anger he always experienced when thinking about them flooded him, making the next step even more difficult.

Lord, help me. Please. Ella needs me.

But the panic threatened to immobilize him. He quaked even more. His breathing became shallow inhalations that left his lungs starving for oxygen-rich air.

Let it go. Forgive.

The conversation he had with Ella took over his thoughts. *As long as I hate them, what they did to me will influence all aspects of my life. Will dominate my actions.*

No! I won't let them.

Time was running out. Every second could be Ella's last. He gritted his teeth and focused on eradicating his hatred, on washing his mind clean, as though he'd been baptized again.

He raised another foot and put it down in front of him. Then another. A faint light ahead drew him in a little farther. Sweat stung his eyes. He swiped the back of his hand across his forehead and pictured Ella's smiling face, her eyes bright with the gleam of mischief.

Then the illumination drawing him into the cave vanished. He halted.

* * *

Ella lay flat on the cave floor, inched forward and felt to see if she could figure out how deep the drop-off was. Reaching down as far as she could, she couldn't touch the bottom.

"I will find you, Ella. You won't escape me this time. Never again."

Keith's words echoed through the cavern, chilling her to the bone.

With a quick glance back, she watched the brightness grow nearer. Although it lit that last bend she'd taken, it wasn't enough to illuminate her surroundings. She began exploring them with her hands, searching for anywhere to conceal herself from Keith. To the side was a large stone. Maybe she could hide behind it and pray he didn't know she'd gone this way.

She crawled behind the rock and curled into the smallest ball she could, sending up her prayers to be saved.

His headlamp washed the area in brightness as though a spotlight was pointing to her hiding place. Her heartbeat pounded against her skull. Her body ached all over, and she couldn't seem to breathe enough.

"Come out. Come out. Wherever you are."

She couldn't even cover her ears to keep from hearing Keith's taunting words. They bombarded her as though he was hammering his fists into her body.

The light came closer. The sound of his breathing seemed to resonate against the rocky walls, drowning out her own thundering heartbeat.

"Gotcha."

Claws grabbed her upper arms and yanked her

from her hiding place, which in the glow barely blocked her from his view. He hoisted her into the air, his bright light glaring in her eyes. Squinting, she peered down. Her legs dangled a few feet off the stone ground. He edged toward the dark drop-off.

"I wonder what's down there, how deep it is."

He held her over the hole. She refused to look and instead stared at his waist.

"Mmm. I can't see the bottom."

He'd put his rifle down and had stuffed his revolver in his belt because his two hands were busy gripping her. As he finally stepped back from the ledge, Ella decided it was now or never.

She shrieked and swung her legs toward him.

A high-pitched blood-curdling cry vibrated through the tunnel. Josiah's grasp on his flashlight tightened. The sound chilled him. He increased his pace. In his gut he knew that was Ella, and she was in trouble.

He rushed around the bend in the cave where the glow had disappeared to a faint then nonexistent illumination. He stumbled over the uneven surface and caught himself before going down. Noises drifted to him. A fight? Although the ground was rugged, with large cracks, he accelerated even more.

"I'm gonna kill you," a gruff masculine voice shouted.

Then the blast of a gunshot, the sound ricocheting off the stone walls in deafening waves. Then another gun went off—different, though. A revolver?

Click. Click. Click, followed by an explosion of words that scorched Josiah's ears. Had the gun stopped working?

He flew over the rough terrain, readying his rifle the best he could one-handed since he held the flashlight in the other. As he neared another curve in the tunnel, he slowed because light shone as though it came from somewhere nearby. He flattened himself against the wall and peeked around the wall into the corridor.

The first thing he saw was Ella racing toward him, a revolver clasped in her handcuffed hands. Then he glimpsed a large, muscular man with blond hair charging Ella, holding a rifle like a club, his face red with rage.

Ella rounded the curve. She spied him and slowed her pace. When she was safe behind him, Josiah thrust the flashlight into her hand, then stepped out into the corridor.

"Stop! Drop your gun," Josiah said, and raised his rifle.

But before he could line up a shot, the tall man kept coming, swinging his gun toward Josiah's head. He crouched and barreled into the blond giant, driving both of them deeper into the tunnel. The man's rifle came down on Josiah's back. Josiah rammed him into the wall. Once. Twice. Until the rifle clattered to the ground.

The giant wrapped his arms around Josiah's torso instead and squeezed so tight that pain stabbed into his chest as if his bruised rib hadn't healed. Josiah brought his hands up and hit the man's ears, hoping to throw him off balance so he would loosen his grip. His arms slackened enough that Josiah broke his hold. Then quickly he moved in and punched one fist into the man's nose and the other into his throat.

The guy staggered back, gasping for air while blood ran down his face. His left foot came down on the edge of a drop-off. He flapped his arms, trying to regain his balance, but before Josiah could reach him, he fell backward. The giant's scream echoed through the cave, followed by a thumping sound.

Panting, Josiah peered down into the hole. The man's light still shone, illuminating his broken body at the bottom of a deep pit.

"Is he dead?" Ella's voice quavered behind him.

Josiah swung around, took one glance at her pale features and wide eyes and drew her away from the drop-off. Then he retrieved the flashlight from her and checked the bottom of the pit again to reassure her that it was over.

When he returned to her, he tugged her against him, trying to absorb the tremors that racked her body. "Yes, he's dead. You're safe now."

"That was Keith. He was going to kill me," she murmured against his chest in a monotone as though she was going into shock.

"Let's get out of here. Into the sunshine. He can't hurt you ever again."

"Are you sure?" A sob tore through her.

"He fell sixty or seventy feet onto a rocky surface, and by the pool of blood around his head, I'm positive."

"Is Robbie all right? He was going to take him." She shuddered.

"He's safe. My sister is guarding him."

When he brought Ella into the sunlight, he sat her down on the ledge and pulled her into the crook of his arm. "When you're ready, we'll hike to the beach to be picked up. Alex and Robbie left in the boat to get help. Then when Keith's body is recovered, you'll have to ID him, and the medical examiner can confirm he's dead."

Ella stood at her living room window as Alex parked her car, hopped out and walked toward her house. For the past two days, since returning from the island, Ella had gone through the motions of living, but a part of her was numb as though she was still in the cave with Keith, listening to him telling her how he was going to kill her.

Earlier she'd talked with her minister, but didn't really think she was free from her ex-husband. She'd thought she was before and he'd found her.

He's dead. Everyone has told me that.

She'd repeated that so many times in the past forty-eight hours she would have thought it would finally sink in. But for so long she had lived in terror, and it wasn't that easy to shake it off.

Maybe when she finally identified his body, she'd be free. No more nightmares for her or Robbie. Was that even possible?

Then her minister's words repeated themselves in her mind. *You won't be free until you forgive Keith. You can't let go while holding on to that kind of hatred.*

Alex rang the doorbell. Ella headed to the foyer to answer it, knowing she had to find the power to forgive.

She forced a smile on her face and greeted Alex. "I'm glad you could take Robbie while I go to ID Keith."

"Sadie is waiting for him to come visit. We'll have fun. Don't hurry to come pick him up. You and Josiah should talk. You haven't had much of a chance since all this happened."

"Do you know if they found Keith's campsite?"

"Yes, I got a call when Josiah landed at the airport. They found it and a stash of firepower that could wipe out a lot of people. Josiah said it looked as though he was planning a small war."

Ella hugged her arms. "A US Marshal came to see me this morning to find out what happened. Apparently my husband left their protection and in the process killed a man. He obviously was very determined to get to me."

"He can't anymore."

"I'm trying to realize that, but he's been such a big part of my life for so long. It's hard to think I'm really free." *Am I really until I finally say that I've forgiven Keith and mean it?*

"Sam and I are ready to go, Alex," Robbie said behind Ella.

"That's great. Sadie's in the car waiting." To Ella she added, "We're going to the park before going to my house. Don't worry about the time you pick him up." Alex looked pointedly at her. "Take care of *all* your business."

"I will."

Robbie threw his arms around Ella. "I love you, Mom."

She ruffled his hair. "I love you, too."

Ella stood in the entrance and watched her son lead his twelve-week-old puppy to Alex's car. She was right about talking with Josiah. She needed to. Once they'd walked out of the woods onto the beach, they hadn't been alone in the midst of Josiah helping with the recovery of Keith's body and the search for his campsite. She'd had her hands full with reassuring Robbie they would be all right and then being interviewed by the authorities about what had happened. A whirlwind forty-eight hours. She desperately wanted her life to return to normal, or rather settle into a new normal. She knew where she would go before she went to ID Keith and see Josiah.

Emotionally and physically drained, Josiah entered the State Medical Examiner's building. He didn't see Ella's Jeep out in the parking lot, so he would wait for her in the lobby. Thomas would be here soon, too.

As he stared out the double glass doors, he realized that now that he'd had time to think, he wanted to move on in his life. Seeing what Ella had gone through for years, all he wanted to do was be there for her and give her a life that would erase her ex-husband from her memories. He'd seen firsthand what anger could do to a person if left to fester and grow. He didn't want that for his life.

As he'd accompanied Thomas and trudged all over the island with Buddy looking for the campsite, they had talked. He'd finally shared his captivity with his best friend. Through Thomas's guidance, he'd given his rage at his captors to the Lord. He never wanted to hate someone so much that he ended up consumed like Keith.

He caught sight of Ella. He held one of the doors open for her, and she entered the building. When she turned toward him, he sucked in a deep breath. She was beautiful inside and out. She gave him hope for the future.

"Are you ready to ID him?" he asked, clasping her hand.

She nodded. "Let's get this over with."

When she saw Keith's face, all she said to the ME was "Yes."

Thomas came into the room as she turned away.

"Thomas, you look as tired as Josiah."

"I've hiked miles the past two days, and I'm ready for a rest. Sorry I'm late. I was turning in the evidence we found at Keith's campsite."

"All Keith said to me was I should have realized I would never escape him completely. He mentioned the story about Seth's rescue at Eagle River and said that I should quit worrying about people besides myself."

"We found a copy of the story written in the newspaper with a photo where you appeared in the background. Not the same one that was on the TV channel. But that had to be how he discovered where you were." Josiah settled his arm on her shoulders.

Thomas frowned. "He bribed an airport employee for David's flight plan that day you all left for the island."

Ella tensed. "Is the employee still alive?"

Thomas's eyes hardened. "Barely. He was left for dead."

Beneath Josiah's arm, she relaxed the tightness in her shoulders. "I'll pray he makes it. Keith liked to tie up loose ends, and I'm glad he didn't succeed here."

"Your ex-husband's death has been ruled an accident. He'll be buried tomorrow. Everything is over,

Ella." Thomas smiled. "Now you two can get on with your lives."

His best friend zeroed in on Josiah's face, his look practically shouting what he meant, especially when he looked back and forth between Ella and Josiah.

"We're leaving," Josiah said. With Ella beside him, he walked into the hallway.

Out in the parking lot, he grasped both of Ella's hands to stop her from getting into her Jeep. "You're a sight for sore eyes, and I really mean sore. I didn't sleep an hour last night. I couldn't rest until any danger of Keith's weapons being found by someone and being used illegally was taken care of." He inched closer. "Now you and I need to talk about our future."

He half expected her to say, "What future?" but she grinned, her eyes bright. She cupped his cheek. "I like the sound of that. I was a little late because I went to church to pray and ask God to help me let go of my anger toward Keith. By the time I left, I felt it lifted from me. He paid the price for his evil. I won't give him the satisfaction of influencing my life for one more second. I want to spend that life with you. I love you."

He brushed his lips over hers and whispered against them, "I love you, too, with all my heart."

Ella wound her arms around him and deepened the kiss. When she finally pulled away, she said, "I'm here for you. I know with help you can move on—"

He pressed his fingers over her lips. "I came to that conclusion when I saw the extremes a person can go to for revenge. It takes over your life and destroys it as much as you want to destroy the other person."

"No matter what, you would never turn into Keith.

You aren't capable of that. You want to help others. He wanted to harm them. You two are worlds apart, and I know that now. For a long time I doubted my ability to really know a person. I thought i did with Keith, and look what happened."

He kissed the tip of her nose. "I want to marry you. We can wait as long as you need, though."

"I don't want to wait any longer. I've been waiting a lifetime for someone like you."

He lifted her against him and swung her around, laughter pouring from him. "Then we aren't waiting anymore. Let's go let Alex and Robbie know to prepare for a wedding soon."

EPILOGUE

Two months later

Josiah put his arm around Ella and approached the elegant restaurant. "We're finally having that special dinner I promised you at Celeste's."

She looked at him, a smile deep in her eyes. "*Special* is the right word. This was the perfect place to have our wedding reception, but you didn't have to buy out the whole place for the night."

"Yes, I did. We have a lot of people who care about us."

When they entered, a sea of familiar faces greeted them with a round of applause and a few loud whistles.

Robbie broke away from Ella's parents, who had come to Alaska for the wedding, and hurried to his mom and hugged her. Then Robbie threw his arms around Josiah. "What took you all so long?"

"You couldn't have been here long. You left the church with your grandparents ten minutes before us." Josiah clasped his shoulder. "Are you going to be all right for a week with your grandparents while your mom and I are away on our honeymoon?"

Robbie grinned. "Yes, I'm going with them to show them the sights of Alaska. I warned them about seeing bears and moose. It didn't seem to bother Grandpa, but Nana isn't so sure about the trip now. Grandpa said that she'd change her mind."

"It's hard to come to Alaska and not see the wonders. I think she'll come around, too."

Robbie signaled for Josiah to lean down, then whispered in a serious voice, "Can I call you Dad now?"

The question stunned Josiah. He'd hoped Robbie would want to one day, but he hadn't expected it so soon. "I'd be honored if you would."

"Thanks, Dad."

"Josiah, we need to greet our guests." Ella touched his arm, the elated look on her face indicating she'd heard what her son had said.

In front of two hundred people, Josiah couldn't resist kissing his wife of an hour. He drew her into his arms and kissed his bride for a second time that night before an audience.

* * * * *

Dear Reader,

To Save Her Child is the second in my Alaskan Search and Rescue series. The state has such contrasts and covers a huge area. Alaska is a great setting for a series centered on search and rescue missions. I've had fun researching different places and scenarios in connection to this story and ones for future books in the series. So many secondary characters are demanding their own stories.

I love hearing from readers. You can contact me at margaretdaley@gmail.com or at PO Box 2074, Tulsa, OK 74101. You can also learn more about my books at www.margaretdaley.com. I have a newsletter that you can sign up for on my website.

Best wishes,

Margaret Daley